# DEAD TO RIGHTS
## by:
## D.S. Cuellar

.22

9mm

Dead to Rights

Copyright 2015 Monarch Moon, LLC
1-2457052161

All rights reserved. No portion of this book may be reproduced or transmitted in any form by any means, electronic or mechanical, without written permission of the publisher.

This is a work of fiction. Names, characters, places, and incidents either are a product of the author's imagination or are used fictitiously, and any resemblance to actual persons, living or dead, business establishments, events, or locales is entirely coincidental.

Cover Photo by
Kei Yoshino of KS Design

*Special Thanks To:*
Paula Sherwood, Bobbie Nelson
Pauline Suite and Marisa Silva-Miller

*Story Editor:*
T. J. Monarch

*Editor:*
Missy Borucki

*Also by: D.S. Cuellar*
Guardian of the Red Butterfly

Please visit the Guardian of the Red Butterfly Facebook page at:
https://www.facebook.com/pages/Guardian-of-the-Red-Butterfly/488388581221928?fref=ts

*Currently working on:*
Guardian of the Monarch Moon

Michael —
What would you do?

D Bugler

.50

# Dead to Rights

A stiff salty breeze had come up and drew a bit of cool air in off the Pacific Ocean. Marisa shifted her feet so the sun baked sand covered them like warm slippers. As Marisa took in the companionship that the perfect summer day had provided, she noticed a man standing on a sand dune about a hundred yards away pointing a camera in her direction. Marisa lifted her camera to her face and focused the high powered lens on him. She watched as he lowered his camera and took a call on his cell phone.

"Hello. Yes, I have an eye on the target."

As Payton was on the phone, he drew a line in the sand with his foot between him and his assignment.

The man on the other end of the conversation was determined to get his point across, "It's my understanding, your precious Kate has made a nice asset to our cause."

Payton took those words to heart as he used his foot to brush away the line in the sand he had just drawn. He realized what they had on him no longer carried any value. Just for an instant as Payton turned and started to walk away, Marisa silently pleaded to the stranger to look back one more time. He did. That's when she rapidly ran off of three consecutive photos. She may not have captured his eyes behind those sunglasses, but he certainly captured her imagination. Marisa wondered if this was the first time he had been to her beach and if he would ever return.

    Payton's mind was focused on one thought, assignment or not, he knew what he had to do. What had all started just over a year ago, his life as he knew it, had changed forever.

**One Year Ago...**

# Chapter 1

"Do you think they're gonna kill us?"

"No. They want something. Most likely details of our assignment."

"Then do you think they're gonna kill us?"

"Remember your training. They're probably going to play us against each other. I will not give you up. Remember that."

They heard the click of the door as someone unlocked it. One of the captors entered, grabbed Kate by the hair, and dragged her out of the door as her screams cut through Payton's heart. He prayed. Years of discipline and brutally intense military training didn't prepare Payton for this—the tactical maneuver of emotional blackmail. He was finding out quickly but unlike other aspects of suffering, Kate's cries were not easily put into a box and stored away. The enemy would play Kate against him and him against her and eventually, one or both of them would do whatever they asked.

Reports of their alleged demise were passed around like propaganda over the airwaves. The rebel forces had captured one of the Army's top sniper teams, Sergeant Gregory Payton and his spotter, Sergeant Kate Devlin. This was their third mission together and although no op is routine, this one was going as planned, find the target and eliminate the threat. As a team, they were always ready for the assigned mission, no questions asked. They had been standing by for two days, waiting as long as it took for their target to arrive, and have a clean shot. It was their job; one they both loved. Assigned to each other as teammates for about a year, in their field of work it was imperative they knew each other well. Audible words could get them killed; minute gestures and expressions kept them alive.

When they took Kate away, the suppressed true feelings Payton felt for her came rushing to the surface. He loved her, not the bonding love of a close partnership or the love above the level of a strong attraction. No, Payton's love for Kate was an internal tourniquet wound so tightly there was no beginning or end. That is what made this so hard for Payton. When they took Kate away, everything he thought he suppressed came rushing to the surface. Another loud cry from Kate and Payton could no longer hold back. "Kate!" he screamed. His plea echoed off of the walls and reverberated in his ears. *Could she hear him?* "Kate!" She had to know that he would never give up on her.

Payton heard sounds from under his door. Heavy boots walking and whimpering were coming closer by the moment. Then what sounded like Kate being dragged across the dirt floor, the grinding of the rusty hinges of the door across from his being opened, and the sound of skin being slapped. Payton could feel Kate's anguish clawing at his heart. After a few more screams from Kate it went silent, like everyone had left Payton alone with his thoughts, none of which were good. From the looks of it, he and Kate were being held in converted storage units. That would account for the dirt floors, poor lighting, and the wide gap under the door.

After long agonizing minutes, someone flipped the latch on the make-shift cell and opened his door allowing Payton to see into the room opposite his where Kate had been taken. She screamed one last time before her captor backhanded her so hard she fell to the ground. Payton saw they had gagged and blindfolded her. He yelled at the guards, "Leave her alone, you fucking cowards.

Leave her alone!" The men laughed then abruptly stopped when two soldiers in faded blue uniforms approached Payton's cell. Their uniforms looked like they hadn't been cleaned in a while. Payton saw grease stains from food on the front of one man's shirt and the uniform of the other man was wrinkled and torn. The two men grabbed Payton off of the dirt floor and threw him into a metal chair that sat in the center of the mid-size room. Payton's back hit the chair; his arms pinned behind him. His hands had been bound for so long, he was losing feeling in his fingers.

    Next a third man entered the room, closing the door behind him. His blue uniform was the cleanest and several service bars were pinned on his shirt pocket. He wore a blue beret over his black greasy hair. Before acknowledging Payton, he barked orders in Spanish at his men. Payton was fairly fluent in Spanish, but he had a hard time understanding exactly what was being said. The man Payton assumed was in charge walked up to him and without warning, backhanded him across his face. His head turned to the side from the force of the blow. If this man had hit Kate with the same force he hit

Payton, he was going to take his time killing this man the moment he had the chance.

"I am General Delgado. As far as your government is concerned, you and the rest of your team are dead. How do I know this you ask? I know this because when the chopper that was sent to pick you up tried to land at your rendezvous point, I had it shot down. Like I said," Delgado threw the file at Payton across the small table before continuing, "your government thinks you are dead." Delgado smiled at Payton, true evil showing in his eyes. He looked at Payton with both eyes and Payton held his stare.

"Now you two are mine. Your survival will be up to you. Your life up to me." Delgado stood and turned his back on Payton, laced his fingers together behind his back, and turned back around to face his new recruit.

"What did you do to Sargent Devlin?" Payton asked holding his breath.

"Oh, you mean your lovely friend, Kate?" Delgado spat at Payton's feet. "Yes, I heard you call out to her." Delgado crouched down until he was face-to-face with Payton and grabbed him by the chin, squeezing with all five fingers. "She will be fine for now. And as long as you do what I say and tell me what I want to know, she'll stay that way." Delgado looked Payton square in the eyes and asked, "Do we have an understanding?"

"Sergeant Payton. U.S. Army Ranger," Payton said proudly refusing to cower before his captor.

Delgado grabbed onto the dog tag that Payton had hanging around his neck, jerked the chain free and with the dog tag still in his hand, backhanded Payton once more. This time drops of blood flew from Payton's mouth as his head was forced to the side. Bringing his eyes back to the General's, the metallic taste of blood touched his tongue.

"First of all, you no longer have any rank here, Alex, and I am in need of a man with your skills. So now, you work for me. Do you understand?" Delgado looked to Payton expectantly. When Payton didn't respond, Delgado turned his back to him once again and said, "I know you are a proud man, and I also know proud men sometimes need convincing." Delgado turned back to face Payton once again, raising his eyebrows waiting for Payton's acquiescence.

Delgado nodded to the two men standing at attention in the corner. Without wasting time, they restrained Payton in the chair as Delgado opened the door. Payton felt the rush of air fill the room as the door was opened. Closing his eyes, he inhaled deeply. When Payton opened his eyes and peered into the next room he could only focus on one thing . . . Kate.

Kate had been stripped of her dignity. There she sat, tied to a wooden chair, completely naked and exposed. They had placed a cloth sack over her head, and her head lolled to the side. She was barely conscious. If it weren't for the ropes tying her hands behind her back and the ones tied around her ankles and knees spreading her legs apart, she would have fallen out of the chair. Payton needed to look away. He couldn't risk these men knowing his true feelings for Kate. But seeing the person he loved the most so vulnerable, he couldn't help but drop his head in shame for her.

"Let her go and I will do whatever job you need done. But first you have to let her go. I mean out of the country, gone!" Payton pleaded still looking down at his lap. He thought if he tried the submissive act the sub-humans holding them captive might let her go, he would do whatever he had to do until the day he killed them or they killed him.

"Why should I believe you?" Delgado spat at Payton's feet pulling Payton's eyes up to meet his. "You haven't proven to me I can trust you." Placing his hand on Payton's shoulder, he said through gritted teeth, "So, I am going to show you what will happen if you fail me."

Kate was thirty feet away yet seemed like a thousand miles. So close, just in the next room, yet she never felt so far away. The rooms they were in were part of a cave system and so the air was naturally regulated to about fifty degrees. Kate sat directly under an intense interrogation lamp. Payton could see her sweating from every pore of her body. Her skin was naturally tanned from the sun, her muscles toned from a job that kept her constantly on the move. Payton couldn't help but look at her exposed body, her perfectly round breasts and rose bud colored nipples. His shame for her noticing her beauty during her suffering nearly killed him right then and there.

≠

Kate regained consciousness and was immediately assaulted by the musty smell of the damp cave. The rank body odor of the men standing next to her nearly made her gag. She could smell their stench through the bag covering her head. She tried to close her legs, but the braided sisal rope pulled at her knees and ankles. She pulled as hard as she could, but the rope just cut into her tender flesh. A wadded up rag they had duct taped into her mouth prevented any sound. Fear as thick as a mud bog suffocated her.

"I'm here, Kate!"

A sound, a voice, a word; Kate listened hard for it again.

"Ka—"

What Kate was listening for had been cut off.

$$\neq$$

Delgado struck Payton in the face again and blocked his view of Kate. He stood, hands resting on his hips in front of Payton. "So you see, Mr. Payton, as long as you do as I say, she will not be harmed," Delgado said as he shifted. "In fact," he continued placing a piece of chewing gum into his mouth, "you two are going to work as a team . . . for me. This will all become clearer as our little training session moves along." Delgado gestured to his men. One man moved in behind Payton and another man stood behind Kate. "This is how it's going to work. You do what I say, complete your assignments, and you will both be rewarded." Delgado moved out of Payton's line of sight. The man behind Kate gathered her long brown hair in his hand, pulling it back to expose her neck. "Who rewards you and how you are rewarded is up to you." Again Delgado motioned to the man behind Kate.

    Payton could see the man's silhouette come into the light, closer to Kate. First he took off his dirty, sweaty shirt and began twisting it around in his hands forming a makeshift rope. The captor then wrapped his shirt tightly around her neck and slowly pulled up on it. Kate started to gag and choke from the lack of oxygen until she blacked out. This pleased Delgado, the corner of his lips lifted in a degraded smile.

    "Stop!" Payton yelled as he released the pent up breath he had been holding for Kate. The large man behind Kate released the shirt from around her neck. Payton waited breathlessly for Kate to regain consciousness. After several minutes she stirred, taking deep breaths. Payton could see the hood over her head billowing as she took a few deep breaths.

Delgado stepped in between Payton and Kate again blocking Payton's view of her. New sounds of torment escaped from Kate's lips as reaction to what must have been her capture groping her. Payton leaned over as far as he could without tilting his chair onto two legs. He stretched his neck to see what these bastards were doing to the woman he loved. It was only a glance. But in that one glance, Payton could see the man behind Kate unbutton and unzip his pants. The rage Payton felt could not be swallowed and just as he was about to say something, Delgado backhanded him across the jaw.

Delgado leaned down into Payton's face, his nasty breath drifting up his captive's nostrils. Grabbing Payton's jaw, he forced him to look into his eyes. "You don't say a word. If you do, my man gets to continue. If you obey, we will let you continue."

Delgado's words didn't register right away. His large form left Payton's line of sight. Payton was left to stare at the man caressing Kate's supple breast. The other guard in her room ran his hand up her thigh, fingering small circles, creeping higher and higher until it rested between her legs. This time Payton did not say a word but met Delgado's gaze with a hatred beyond measurement.

# Chapter 2

"Good. I see you are a fast learner, Mr. Payton. You have chosen to cooperate. That is good for everyone concerned and, for that, you will be rewarded."

Delgado motioned to the men groping Kate. The men stopped, immediately pulling their hands off of her. Payton breathed a sigh of relief. Thank God. But his relief was short lived when each man retrieved a pistol from their side holsters and pointed them directly at Kate's head.

Suddenly, the man behind Payton took out a knife and shoved Payton forward. Using the knife in a quick, upward movement, he cut Payton's hands free, grabbed Payton by the head, and placed the knife to Payton's throat resting the sharp blade against his jugular.

"One false move, my friend, and our friend, Kate, will wish she was dead by the time my men get done with her," Delgado warned, a smile playing on his lips.

Payton nodded. For Kate, he would cooperate. This would be alright. He would find a way for both of them to get out of this if it was the last thing he did.

One of Delgado's men dropped an old, worn-out twin mattress on the dirt floor in front of Kate's chair. The man guarding Payton helped Payton over to the mattress because his feet were still tied together then shoved him to his knees in front of Kate. The man behind Kate, whose pants were still unbuttoned, removed the hood from her head. At first the light was too bright but a few blinks to clear the sweat from her eyes allowed her to focus on Payton kneeling in front of her.

"Payton, what's going on?" she asked frightened and confused.

One of the guards who had his gun pointed at Kate's head turned and pointed it at Payton.

"No!" Kate yelled as the adrenaline from the situation kicked in.

Unable to speak, he shook his head and closed his eyes as he prayed for her to be quiet. His motions and movements Kate understood. They were long past the point of words. Kate knew what Payton was asking. She remained tight-lipped.

Delgado provided the explanation Kate didn't need. "What Payton is trying to say, Kate, is that he cannot speak to you. He knows if he does, we will kill you. Clearly he cares for you and is willing to do just about anything to keep you alive." Delgado continued on, hands braced against his hips. His was a position of authority. El general needed to make certain that both Kate and Payton knew exactly who was in charge. Getting Payton to be silent was the first step in his scheme. "As you can see by this report," Delgado thrust the report under the bright lights and waited for Kate's eyes to focus on the words. "Even your own government has given up on." Delgado smirked at Kate.

"No, that's not true. I'm sure there is a team out there right now looking for us," Kate said on baited breath. Surely someone was looking for them. They couldn't have just given up on their best sniper team. She thought back to their last reported location. Delgado had captured them, and they had traveled all night. The Army would have no way of finding them. If they were to get out of this, it would have to be without support.

"Look right here, Kate. Look at the top of this report," Delgado placated her. "Look right here where it says in big, bold letters: Missing-In-Action. You are missing. They have no idea where you are."

"Then just go ahead and kill me. Get it over with." Kate was done playing games. She didn't want to see Payton hurt. That would be a fate worse than death.

Kate's words were a shock to Payton's whole being. At that very moment his whole world was sitting right in front of him. He could not let Kate see his love for her. Tears: big, bad, nasty tears began to flow from his heart.

"Payton. It's okay. Let me go," Kate whispered.

Payton communicated to Kate with just a look that he would never let her go. Kate bowed her head. She understood Payton. She understood what his eyes were screaming at her. He would never let her go. She knew that. She knew he would die protecting her.

Delgado knew he had what he wanted: two highly skilled assassins at his beck and call. "Now for the entertainment," Delgado thought as he looked first at Kate and then at Payton, both helpless and bound for him.

"Release the girl from the chair," Delgado commanded. The man rushed to release Kate, quickly untying her legs, ankles, and finally her hands.

"Do what I say. When I say it. That way we can get on with what we need to do. What you were trained to do. Only now, you will be working for me. Do you understand, Kate?" Delgado asked as he brushed the back of his hand over her naked breast. Kate flinched.

"Never," Kate spat the venomous word at her captor.

"If you don't want to play, that's fine. I will slowly kill your friend, Payton. Right. In. Front. Of. You. And then my men will take turns taking their frustrations out on you. You never know, you might even enjoy it," Delgado said as he rolled her nipple between his thumb and forefinger. "However they please," he grinned.

Kate's heart pounded in her chest as she realized that she was naked and Payton was seeing her this vulnerable. She could see it plainly on his face, in his eyes, he loved her. She knew this as she knew she would take another breath. He never told her. She had her own secrets she was keeping from Payton. She had always wished that they would be more, more than friends, more than Shadow Team partners. Being a professional, she never let herself act on the feelings she now knew she shared with Payton. But now, she knew, he too had been holding back his true feelings for her. Leaning against his forehead, she rested her head.

"I understand now," she whispered, her breath caressing his face.

Payton opened his eyes and looked into her big brown eyes. Without saying a word, he told her he loved her, and her eyes reflected the love that he felt. He knew she got the message.

"Let's not stop there," Delgado said excitedly wanting to see his entertainment.

Delgado wrapped his hand in her long hair and pulled Kate down onto the old mattress. She laid there, on her side, in the fetal position. Slowly, while he met Kate's gaze, he undid his belt and took it off. He looped it and placed it around her neck. He held onto the other end like a master holding the leash to his faithful dog while one of the guards tied her feet together.

"Get up on your knees, Kate," Delgado commanded.

She hesitated at first, but when the guard holding the pistol on Payton racked his slide on his weapon, she started to move. Delgado pulled on the belt as if helping her, but it was more for a show of power . . . for Payton's sake. Kate made it up to her knees as best she could with her hands still tied behind her back. Delgado forced her head to the mattress leaving her hips up in the air, exposed. Kate felt the grime from the filthy mattress against her face. She smelled a musky, dirty stench that permeated the mattress. She tried to hold as still as possible so to touch as little of the bloodstained mattress as she could.

    The guard watching over Payton cracked his pistol over the back of Payton's neck. He forced Payton, while on his knees, to move in behind Kate. One of the guards reached under Payton to unbutton and unzip his pants. Then, the same guard yanked down his pants and then his underwear past his buttocks.

    "This is how we are going to reward you," Delgado grinned with delight that his plan was working. "When I give you an assignment and you execute it properly and in a timely manner, she will be your reward." Delgado brought his fingers together and steepled them. He looked into Payton's eyes with a fierceness Payton had yet to witness. "If you are late or fail your assignment, then one of my men will take your place and reap the benefits of your reward." Delgado kneed Payton in the back making his hips touch Kate's rear.

"And for every thirty minutes you are late, another one of my guards will have his way with our lovely Kate here," Delgado said as he bent over and stroked Kate's hair in a soothing manner. "Do I make myself clear, Payton?"

Payton, still unable to speak, simply nodded.

"You have a choice to make, Payton. Either take your reward now, or I will," Delgado said as he let up on the leash. "My sweet, Katie," Delgado said palming her ass. "Unlike Payton, you, my dear, can scream out whatever your little heart desires."

Suddenly, Payton felt the tip of a long knife at his back and the prodding made his body jump forward. Then another jab. He knew he would not let Kate die as much as he wished this nightmare was over. Payton began to feel his body tighten and the sheer thought of having to perform for these animals had him shaking uncontrollably. He couldn't do it. Not like this. Payton could hear the rush of blood in his ears.

Delgado's voice broke the silence. "I'll tell you what, Payton. Let's leave it up to Kate. Kate, what do you say? Do you feel it is time to be rewarded?"

Her silence spoke volumes. She didn't want to give into these bastards any more than Payton did.

"I see," Delgado said as he looked adoringly at Kate lying on the mattress, ass still up in the air for the taking. "Let's give you both a little time to think about it."

"Put him back. Tie him up. Gag him. Face his chair so he has to stare at her," Delgado barked his commands. Before putting Payton back in the chair, the men pulled down Payton's underwear and pants all the way to his ankles. They wanted to disgrace him in front of Kate. Next, the men tied Kate up by her out-stretched hands, over her head, so tight, her tip toes touched the ground.

Delgado removed his belt from around Kate's neck and wrapped one end securely in his grip. The slap of the belt landing flush against Kate's back was the worst sound Payton had ever heard. He felt her pain but knew it was nothing compared to what she was feeling. She was able to keep from screaming by biting on her bottom lip so hard she drew blood. But when the next lash landed against her buttocks, her scream was uncontrollable and excruciating. Her body twisted and writhed enough for Payton to see the welts forming on her ass cheeks in the shape of the end of the belt. Payton could even see where the notches in the end of the belt must have been. Her body was weak. They both had been kept awake for over twenty-four hours. Her body was giving in. *But was her mind?* He could see her strength leaving her body as a small stream of blood ran down along the curve of her ass cheeks, along her thigh from where the lashing had torn the flesh from her buttock.

When Delgado had seen her body give in, he knew she was his. He could and would use her as he pleased to control Payton. So for today, this was enough. He cut her down and carried her over to the mattress on the floor and laid her down gently. All Payton could do was look at her and weep.

# Chapter 3

What seemed like forever was only an hour as Payton was left alone to look at Kate passed out on the floor, still bound and naked. Payton heard Delgado whistling as he entered the room. He had brought a tray of food and water. Behind him, one of the guards had brought a bucket of warm water, a couple of towels, wash clothes, and a much needed blanket. The guard untied Payton's hands and the two men left the room. Payton untied his feet and the ropes that held Kate. He got the wash cloth wet and began to wash her face, hoping to revive her. He used the moisture in the wash cloth to slowly drip across her lips. He squeezed the water out of it, and her lips began to move. He let her suck on the wet towel to get moisture onto her tongue so she could talk. "Kill me. Don't let them do this. Let them kill me. Payton please," she begged.

Her request left Payton feeling helpless. He loved this woman. "I can't, Kate. I can't," he pleaded with her to understand.

Payton spent the next half hour washing her, feeding her, and then putting her to bed. While she slept, he took the time to wash himself and eat. He lay down next to her and wrapped his arms around her. He wanted, more than anything, to make her feel safe. He could hear her shallow breaths. He could feel his heart pounding. He knew he was in love with this woman, and as he held her, he realized he had been for a long time.

They couldn't have been asleep for more than a couple of hours when the door flew open and Delgado's men rushed in to take Kate once more. As Payton reached for her, he felt a boot catch him flush on the ribs knocking the wind out of him. The next session had begun.

Payton once again found himself forced to watch the guards follow out Delgado's orders. This time they wrapped a towel around Payton's genitals and ran jumper cables from the towel to a car battery placed at Payton's feet. Payton could feel a low hum pass through the towel but it wasn't enough to hurt him. But he also knew the bucket of water the guard was holding was meant for him. *Delgado was stepping up his game.*

"Kate, when you are ready, we will begin. You can either be rewarded right here, right now, or we can see just how much pain our friend, Payton can take.

Kate hated the way he said "Our friend." It made her so angry. She wanted to use that anger to hold out, but at the same time, she didn't want to see Payton go through any pain because of her. "Okay, you can have me," she conceded. Delgado smiled brightly. His dark blue eyes sparkled.

"My dear, I already have you," Delgado said with a solemn look in her direction. "Now it is about doing what is asked of you and doing it in a timely manner. I am afraid this is taking much too long," Delgado said as he walked closer to Payton. Kate's eyes followed his movements. She could see the battery and started to worry.

The guard moved closer to Payton with the water bucket. Kate could no longer hold back her emotions for Payton. "No! Don't! I will do whatever you ask," she begged, but her cries fell on deaf ears.

"I'm sorry my dear, Kate. I don't believe you." Delgado nodded to the guard with the bucket who quickly doused Payton with the water. Almost instantly the water soaked Payton and the towel that was between his legs. The current from the battery began to pass through the wet towel shocking Payton as the current rode up his wet torso, electrocuting him. His thighs were convulsing like a frog's legs in a junior high school science class experiment. A spark shot off the battery as some of the water that was flowing over Payton hit the hot battery. The guard kicked off one end of the jumper cables, effectively ending the obedience session.

Kate, seeing Payton's body convulsing, began to cry. Every muscle in her own body began to tighten as if she too was going through the same pain.

Delgado knew he could get to Payton through Kate, but he saw something in Kate that he wanted for himself. "Get these two animals out of my sight," Delgado commanded as he pointed to the opposite room.

One set of guards took Payton away to a holding cell and another set took Kate to a cell opposite Payton's. They both had been stripped of all their clothes and were made to sleep on the dirt floors. In the darkness they had both lost all track of time.

The guards varied their mealtimes as a way to keep them disoriented. Kate's mind began to wander, and she hadn't even noticed her cell door was wide open. She used the wall to help herself to get to her feet, then she made her way over to the doorway. In the hall between her cell and Payton's was a table. Sitting at one end was Delgado.

"Hello, Kate. Would you like to join me?" Delgado asked as he steepled his fingers and brought them below his mouth.

Kate could hardly focus as she slowly walked over to the table and sat down.

"Where's Payton?" she asked cautiously. She didn't want to be the reason for anymore of Payton's pain.

"Let's not talk about that right now. Let's talk about this report. As you can see, you're still missing."

The problem was, Kate could barely see anything at all. Between the low light, lack of food, and lack of sleep, most everything was a blur like the rest of her mind. Delgado handed her the report, but all Kate could make out were the three large letters in bold type at the top of the page: M. I. A.

Delgado continued to taunt her. "Can I get you something to eat?" Delgado lifted a lid off of a platter that was in the middle of the table displaying a whole roasted chicken. The aroma alone took her back home where she remembered cooking with her mother as a child. She used that loving memory to let Delgado know she wasn't his. "No. Not unless we can share it with Payton. Where is he?"

Delgado smiled. He loved the fight in her. "I tell you what. Why don't I let you and Payton cleanup first and then we will talk about it. How does that sound?" Delgado asked faking concern he didn't feel.

The water pressure from the fire hose was so intense that it felt like one continuous prod with the end of a baseball bat. The guard seemed to take pleasure in hosing down the two prisoners. Payton tried his best to stand in the way of the spray to protect Kate from taking a direct shot from the hose. Just when they thought it was over, Kate fell and landed in the mud at their feet. Payton did his best to help her up, but the guard stepped in even closer adding more pressure and knocking Payton over on top of Kate. The guard momentarily turned off the hose and allowed Payton to help Kate back to her feet. The guard cracked open the valve once again and hosed them down.

"That's enough!" Delgado ordered and the guard shut down the hose.

The prisoners were hauled off to their cells, but this time, they were taken to the same cell. Payton must be dreaming because in the middle of dirt floor sat a mattress with two blankets on it.

Payton knew that Delgado wanted Kate for himself, and Payton had been biding his time, waiting to have this moment with Kate to plan their escape. Not only were they left the mattress, but Delgado also turned on the light in their cell. It wasn't much, but because their cell was so small, the heat from the light seemed to take the chill out of the air.

Payton could see the light wasn't going to be enough to warm up Kate. He laid down one of the blankets on the mattress to cover the filth and then helped Kate onto the blanket. He lay down next to her and covered both of them with the remaining blanket. He could feel her body shivering next to his, and he wrapped his arm around her midsection. For Payton, everything about Kate was at a distance. The way they worked together; she has his spotter. They both were always looking down range, a mile away, and now he couldn't feel any closer to her. He could feel the chemistry that they had and the warmth that was being generated between them. He could feel how soft her skin felt pressed against him. He could feel her in his arms as her breathing softened and she began to relax. He could feel her fall asleep. He never felt closer to her than at that exact moment. He didn't know how long this feeling would last, but he did know for now, it was everything. Knowing how much he cared for Kate and the closer they became, the stronger his feelings for her grew. That made it harder for him to leave her if he had to, to save her life. That was his last thought as he closed his eyes and fell asleep alongside her to the rhythm of their beating hearts.

Kate had fallen asleep on Payton's arm. With the adrenaline pumping through his system along with his feelings for Kate and fearing for her safety, Payton could not sleep. He felt Kate snuggle back into his body as she pressed herself back into him. Payton ran his fingertips along her waist, following the curves along her hip. He kissed her shoulder, tasting her, not knowing if she was fully awake. At that moment, there was nothing that could taste any better than her.

Payton felt himself getting firmer as every part of his body that was in contact with hers seemed to double in sensitivity and awareness. As much as he wanted her, he tried to control himself. He tried to lean back and put some space between them but stopped when he felt her hand reach back and grab a hold of his hip.

Kate dug her nails into his flesh and pulled him back into her as she whispered, "Payton, hold me. Don't let go."

Payton could feel his heart beating feverously inside his chest. He felt the electricity between them arc. For the first time, she acknowledged his feelings for her. All of his senses rose to another level with Kate in his arms. Feeling powerful and heady, he moved her hair to the side and brought his dry, hot mouth to her neck to quench his thirst. Each kiss the key to releasing her from this captivity. His comfort guided her through the maze her heart was lost in. Payton took Kate's hand in his and drew their joined hands across her body to her supple breasts. Together, they felt every curve that made up her firm yet tender angelic body. Payton began slowly grinding his hips back and forth as he found the pleasure of brushing up behind her euphoric. Payton moved their hands down to Kate's center.

"Kate..." Payton began.

He was just about to express his love for her when she whispered, "Shhhh." Kate turned her head back just enough to look Payton in his aqua blue eyes. At that moment, Payton would have done anything she asked. "Take me away from here, Payton. Just love me," she pleaded.

Kate drew their hands down across her stomach and pressed Payton's hand between her thighs, grinding herself over his hand. He could feel her wetness. As he entered her, they both moaned their pleasure for one another as they enjoyed the feeling they both had been dreaming of for so long. They grinded in rhythm as Kate arched her back allowing Payton to go deeper with each thrust.

For Payton, the intensity was overwhelming. He too escaped with her. The heat between them was a fire that was sent from heaven as they both could feel their sweat running together and down over their glistening bodies. Payton held Kate in his arms and together they rode out the wave of her climax followed shortly by his. As a shiver continued to run through her body, Kate's legs began to quiver with the pleasure Payton had provided.

Coming back down for Payton was intense because he realized this might be their only time together as lovers. He tried to fight the reality seeping back into his mind. Concerned for Kate, he wanted to ask her, to tell her, to express to her the depth of his feelings. But then he thought better of it. He would allow her to have this moment. He placed gentle kisses on the back of her neck. He stroked her soft, dark hair. Without a word, he let her fall back asleep in the safety and warmth of his arms.

# Chapter 4

Sleep eluded Payton. As tired as he was, his senses seemed to be slowly coming back and with that, a plan. A way out for both of them. He knew if he could just get Delgado alone, he could overtake him and use him as a hostage to bargain for Kate's release. He knew he would only have one chance. He kissed Kate's shoulder, nipping and sucking as he went. Hating to wake her, he had to discuss the plan with her.

"Kate. Wake up. We need to talk," Payton cooed gently into her ear. She began to stir in his arms. Rolling over, she met his cool blue eyes. "I have a plan," he said and explained what he aimed to do.

"What are you going to use for a weapon?" Kate asked trailing her fingertips up and down Payton's muscular arms.

"Anything I can get my hands on. I'm going to have to improvise until I can get his gun away from him," he said as he drew small circles around her areola.

"Then what?" Kate asked anxiously.

"I'll come back for you, and we'll get the hell out of here."

"Where is here? We don't even know where we are, or what this place is?"

"As far as I can tell, it looks like a way station for guns, narcotics, and cash. I keep seeing the same guards over and over, so I think there aren't too many here. Are you strong enough to run?" Payton asked meeting her dark eyes.

"Yes. I would rather die out there than at the hands of these bastards."

"That's my girl. Use that anger. Let's get some distance between us and this place as fast as we can. With any luck, we might be able find a vehicle we can borrow."

"Delgado has a jeep ready to go. I was there when he sent one of his men to go fuel up. He also has a sat phone we can use to call in a strike," Kate replied animatedly.

Their conversation was cut short as they heard a key unlock their cell door. Two of Delgado's guards entered the room. One immediately drew his weapon on Payton. The other tossed Kate a cheaply made, used summer dress.

"Put that on. The General wants you to join him for dinner," the guard said as he spat his chewing tobacco on the floor next to the mattress.

Kate stood up clutching the dress to her chest in an effort to protect what little dignity she had left. She looked to Payton. Her eyes pleading with his. The two guards grabbed Payton under the arms and yanked him from the floor. They started to drag him out the door. Just as Payton reached the threshold, he mouthed the words "I love you" to Kate. He saw a lone tear fall onto her cheek before the bastards dragged him completely out of the room.

When Kate finally emerged from the cell, she saw Delgado at one end of the table and that the guards had tied Payton to a chair at the opposite end of an eight-foot, wooden table.

"Why, Kate, don't you look lovely this evening. Please, join us," Delgado said motioning for her to take a seat. Like she really had a choice.

Kate walked from her cell doorway toward the end of the table to sit down next to Payton, but Delgado had other plans.

"Kate." Delgado slid out the chair next to him. Kate slowly walked back to Delgado's side. As she did so, she noticed that there was enough food on the table for ten people. She also noticed the bottles of wine.

"Who else will be joining us?" Kate asked boldly looking down at her feet.

"This is all for you, Kate. I want to make sure you had a choice. I even picked out a nice Chardonnay and a bottle of Cabernet Sauvignon to go with our meal," Delgado said with a partially chewed cigar stuck in between his strong fingers.

"No, thank you." Kate didn't want to partake in whatever it was Delgado had planned. Although the food did smell good, and she was so hungry.

"Are you sure? I think you should try this Cabernet. It is from a local vineyard," Delgado said as he motioned for the guard to uncork the wine. As the guard moved away from Payton, he holstered his weapon. Payton, being the trained, observant man that he was, did not let this detail go unnoticed.

Payton had to count on their nonverbal communication. He locked eyes with Kate and then slowly looked to the guard's holstered weapon. Kate looked too. Even though Payton was gagged, he knew she got the message. The guard poured the wine for Kate, then Delgado, and then returned to his post behind Payton. Delgado picked up his glass of wine and held it out towards Kate.

"Salute."

Kate picked up her glass by the stem, tapped the rim of her glass to Delgado's, and did her best to play along as she took a sip.

"There," Delgado mocked, "that wasn't so bad."

Delgado began to serve Kate.

"What can I get you? We have pollo, pescado, and carne asada. Which would you prefer?" Delgado asked holding the serving spoon in his hand, his partially chewed cigar setting in an ashtray on the corner of the table.

Kate was so hungry, and she knew this may be the last meal she was going to have for a long time, so she chose the blandest of the three that she thought her stomach could handle. She chose the roasted chicken over the fish and what looked like some sort of barbecue. As they ate in silence, Kate tore off a nice chunk of white breast meat with her fingers. Delgado wasn't stupid enough to provide her with silverware.

Savoring the flavor, she sipped her wine to cleanse her pallet. Delgado watched her hungrily. He watched her place delicate bites into her mouth, cleansing her pallet between each bite. It pleased him to see her take pleasure in her food.

Without saying a word, she stood up, and walked over to Payton's end of the table. She knew, no matter what Delgado said, she was going to share her meal with Payton. Delgado, trying to gain Kate's trust, allowed her to feed Payton. As Kate removed the gag from Payton's mouth, the guard put his hands on Payton shoulders, and held him down in his seat. Kate pulled apart a piece of chicken from the breast meat. She used her fingers to place it into Payton's mouth. Delgado did not like this, but he let her continue. Encouraging their feelings for one another would ensure two highly trained assassins willing to do whatever they had to save the other's life.

As Kate felt Payton's lips close around the tips of her fingers, they looked into each other's eyes. Their moment wasn't over. She fed him another bite, but something in Payton's eyes had changed. He was no longer looking at her with love and passion. Instead, he was looking at her with need and urgency. She knew it was now or never. Kate went back for her glass of wine and brought the glass to Payton's lips. When she was done, she left her glass on the table in front of Payton before she returned to her seat.

Delgado looked at Kate's wineglass then nodded to the guard. The guard removed the glass from in front of Payton and brought it back, placing it next to Kate's plate. As Delgado refilled Kate's glass, the guard took his station behind Payton.

"My dear, Kate. I gave you what you asked for, a nice meal with Payton. Now I want you to give me what I want." Delgado smiled sweetly, sickeningly with a cigar hanging from his lips. He grabbed Kate's chair by the seat and dragged it closer to him. "And what I want is for you and Payton to work for me. It's that simple. I will give Payton an assignment, and if he returns on time, I will give you two some alone time. If he fails the assignment or is late, my men will be happy to take his place," Delgado said bringing the lighter up to his cigar. He took two long puffs giving Kate and Payton a moment to think. "Here is the deal. I send Payton out with an assignment, and you stay here with me. If Payton doesn't complete his assignment and return here on time, my men are going to exact punishment on you. What do you think Payton? Sound fair?" Delgado puffed on his cigar, the pungent odor nauseating Kate.

Kate looked around the table for anything she could use as a weapon. She knew she didn't have much time and looked to Payton for help. The tension was ripe and thick in the room. There was no way Payton would allow this. She noticed Payton look to the salt-and-pepper shakers on the table.

"Kate?" Delgado's voice and the smoke from the cigar adding to the tension in the room. Kate swallowed down the bile that was rising in the back of her throat. She couldn't breathe.

Kate did not know what it was, Delgado's voice or the wine, but all of a sudden she couldn't move. Then it began. It was very subtle at first, a tremor running through her body. Then she began to tremble all over. Delgado knew he had her just where he wanted her. She was ready to break, and all that it was going to take was one final statement; a statement of complete control. Delgado slid the missing in action report in front of Kate.

"Pick it up," Delgado demanded.

Even Payton noticed Kate was unaware of her own trembling. It was as if she was frozen in time. Delgado reached under the table and grabbed Kate's leg firmly. "I said, pick it up," Delgado commanded through gritted teeth.

Kate may not have been aware of her own trembling, but she did feel Delgado's grip on her thigh. What she didn't feel should have scared her. Although he was squeezing hard, she felt no pain. It was as if her leg, her whole body had fallen asleep. Numb. Kate picked up the document and all she could focus on where the three letters in bold type: M-I-A. Kate turned as if in slow motion and looked at Delgado. Delgado noticed Kate's eyes did not hold a passion for life they once did. Her body was there but her spirit was gone.

Delgado knew he had her at her most vulnerable. He knew it was his time to make her his puppet. His puppet to dangle in front of Payton in order to control him. Delgado motioned to the guard to clear away the plates at his end of the table. He took the document from Kate and laid it on the table directly in front of her. The big, bold letters M. I. A. staring her in the face. He took

Kate by the hand and slid his chair away from the table. "Come here my sweet, Kate," Delgado said as he smiled to Kate. He pulled her closer to his body.

Kate, as if in a trance, stood and then moved over in front of her captor. Delgado began to caress her legs as if adding the finishing touches to the woman he had created. As his hands moved higher under her dress, all Payton could do was watch. Payton tried to turn his head, but the guard held it in place with both hands.

Delgado's hands reached the top of her thighs and with a gentle nudge, he pressed her back against the edge of the table. As he stood, Kate could feel his hands run up her dress until he was able to gently lay her back onto the table. Delgado pinned her arms above her head and held them there indicating for her not to move them. She didn't fight him. She could feel Payton's eyes on her. She wanted to reach out for him, but Payton had never felt further away.

Delgado had been waiting for this moment. He brought his hands around Kate's body and took delight in caressing her beautiful, firm breasts. He wedged his body in between Kate's knees, forcing her to expose herself to him. Delgado could feel the adrenaline running through him, stimulating his prowess, his desire for Kate building in him like a wildfire. He brought his hands down across her body to her hips. Brushing one hand over the dark hair that formed a perfect triangle over her mound, Delgado was ready to claim his prize.

Payton tried to look away but the guard had a firm grasp of his hair and forced him to watch Delgado turn his beloved Kate into his sex slave. Payton knew the penalty for talking but could not hold back. "Kate," he cried, his voice echoing off of the walls.

Kate wanted to cry out to Payton but was unable to as Delgado grabbed the chain that held her dog tag around her neck and pulled it up to one side as tight as he could without breaking, cutting off her air. She reached out toward Payton's voice. As the guard was distracted placing the gag in Payton's mouth and Delgado was unbuttoning his pants, Kate felt the back of her hand knock over the salt shaker. Kate grabbed the shaker and cupped it, hiding it in her hands.

Just when she thought she had a window of hope, her world was turned upside down. She felt Delgado thrust himself inside her. With each thrust, Kate shuddered in pain. Delgado didn't care how it felt for

Kate as he ripped the chain from off her neck and tossed the dog tag to the floor. Kate took a deep breath and as she let out a moan of pain, Delgado felt her body gasp as well and he knew with each thrust he was taking her soul. He knew he was going to break her just like he had once broken a wild stallion. He grabbed the document and shoved it in Kate's face. With each thrust, he drove his point home. "You. Are. Mine. Kate. You. Are. Mine."

After all the torture, starvation, and humiliation, Kate's mind knew the only way she was going to survive was to escape. He may have taken her body, but her mind was willing to fight, even if she was no longer Kate.

"Mia," Kate grunted with Delgado's thrust.

"What's that, Kate? I can't hear you," Delgado exhaled with a heavy breath.

Kate's body knew the only way she could fight back was to take on a different persona. The last name to register with her was spelled from the bold letters of the Missing-In-Action report: M. I. A. She whispered, "Mia."

Delgado leaned in, kissed Kate on the lips, and as they parted he heard what Kate was saying. Again, Kate grunted, "Mia."

Delgado saw the document lying off to the side of Kate's shoulder. He saw the bold lettering and saw that his Kate was now his Mia. This seemed to energize him even more. His thrusts became deeper, and his Mia began to accept him. He felt her legs wrap around him and grip on to his body. "Oh, I see we have a new player. Nice to meet you, Mia," Delgado grunted as he pounded in to her. Each thrust bringing him to a new level of pleasure. He liked breaking his toys.

What Delgado couldn't foresee was that his Kate may not have been willing to fight back and jeopardize Payton, but Mia was. Delgado also didn't realize that as he was kissing Kate, Mia had removed the lid from the salt shaker and had emptied it into her hand. Mia taunted Delgado. "Oh, El general," she moaned as she gripped him tighter with her legs.

Delgado could not resist one more kiss from his precious Mia. As he leaned in, Mia gripped her legs tightly around Delgado. She threw her handful of salt directly into Delgado's wide-opened, surprised eyes. The instant pain and shock to his system caused him to pause just long enough for Mia to grab the wineglass and snap away the cup from its stem. Without hesitation, Mia sat up and shoved the long shard of glass deep into the trapezius muscle that ran between Delgado's shoulder and neck. Everything happened so fast, the guard didn't have time to register the circumstances. Payton seized his opportunity. He threw his chair back into the guard pinning him to the dirt floor. Payton tried as hard as he could to keep his weight on top of the guard, but the guard pushed Payton to the side, stood, and drew his weapon on Payton.

Two shots rang out. But they weren't from the guard's weapon. Mia had managed to get the .45 from Delgado's holster. Without hesitation, she put two rounds in the guard's head. He was dead before he hit the floor. Delgado, regaining composure, screamed in anger, "You Bitch!"

Just as Mia turned the weapon on Delgado, another guard came rushing into the room, weapon drawn. Mia was ready. She already had a bead on him and with two quick pulls of the trigger, dropped him in his tracks. A second guard entered, again he was too late as he was not expecting the woman to be holding a gun.

"Kate, help get me out of this chair," Payton yelled.

As Delgado was fighting off the effects of the salt in his eyes, Mia went over to Payton and untied his hands.

"Let's go, Kate," Payton said tugging on her hand.

Mia was now torn between the affection she felt in Payton's voice and the safety of remaining in her new persona.

Delgado watched through semi-conscious eyes as Payton took Kate by the wrist and pulled her out the room and into the tunnel. Delgado used the edge of the table and pulled himself to his feet and more importantly, to his radio. "Stop the hostages," Delgado commanded as he applied pressure to his neck wound with his left hand. Blood seeped between his fingers and ran onto the dirt floor.

Stopping Kate in the tunnel, Payton grabbed her by the hand and looked deep into her eyes. "Are you sure about the Jeep?"

"Yes. I saw him toss the keys to the guard and heard him tell the guard to fill it up and have it ready."

"Okay. It looks like there is light at the end of this tunnel. When we hit daylight, it's going to be hard to see so I want you to stay right on my six, but we have to make it to that jeep. Just run as hard as you can. Can you do that?" Kate didn't respond. Instead she looked away from Payton's worried gaze.

"I said, can you do that? Do you think you can make it to the Jeep as I lay down cover fire?" Payton asked shaking her gently by the shoulders.

Mia nodded.

Payton checked the clip in the .45 and saw that he had five rounds and one in the port. "Okay, Kate. Here we go." Payton reached for her hand and squeezed it in a reassuring manner. They began a slow trot through the tunnel towards the light. Just before the exit, Payton gripped Kate's hand. Hearing his heart beat in his ears, he started running as fast as he could with Kate in tow. As they reached the exit, the light blinded their eyes. Payton's reflexes brought his gun hand up to shield his eyes from the sunlight. But all it did was leave him defenseless to Delgado's men who were waiting for them. Ten guards, all carrying rifles which were now pointed at them.

What they thought was an exit was actually an entrance to a much larger space, a staging area. They had stumbled into a cache of weapons, cocaine, and cash.

It didn't take long for Payton's eyes to adjust and see that there was nowhere to go. For Kate's safety, Payton stayed rooted to his spot. One of the guards walked up and took the .45 from Payton's hand and walked back the way Payton and Kate had just come. When Payton looked over his shoulder, he stood in disbelief. Delgado was walking in their direction. In his right hand was the glass stem from the wineglass. The guard tried to hand Delgado his .45, but Delgado dismissed the gun with a wave of his hand. He stalked towards Payton. Standing one foot in front of Payton, Delgado used his anger and pain to knee Payton right between the legs. Falling to his knees, the pain momentarily crippled him.

Delgado closed the distance between himself and Kate in two strides. Grabbing Kate by her hair, he twisted his hand into her long strands. He pulled her head back by her hair and looked directly into her eyes. "I have an assignment for you, Payton. Good news is, it's back in the states. I'm sending you home." Delgado's eyes sparkled as he watched Mia's expression morph into one of confusion and hope. Never breaking eye contact, Delgado continued, "I am giving you one week to complete your assignment. And if you don't. . ." Delgado held the glass shard by the round bottom of the glass and with one quick movement, shoved it into Kate's thigh. "I'm going to keep Kate for myself."

Mia dropped silently to the ground in front of Payton. She wouldn't give Delgado the satisfaction of her screams. She looked into Payton's eyes trying to take her mind off of the pain.

Payton's anger raged. "And if I get the job done in less than a week?" Payton challenged through gritted teeth.

"It's simple," Delgado retorted, "Kate lives."

# Chapter 5

Present Day

"I'm a dead man," Robert Westmore said, his words sounded like a statement of inconvenience. Using a pair of high-powered binoculars, he looked past his own reflection that was mirrored in the dirty window to scrutinize the scene down below.

"Isn't that what you wanted?" Daniela Figari asked as she lounged on the bed smoking a cigarette. The strikingly beautiful, natural redhead was Robert's occasional play toy and involuntary confidant. "What's next isn't going to be easy, is it?" Smoke trailed in waves after her words.

"That's why I have Payton," Robert said never moving his eyes from the scene below.

"Like you have me?" Daniela spoke with hopeful confidence.

"No, you I took. Payton I made," Robert said as pride touched his chest. He was a major player in the business world and had the perfect cover. The people and opportunities around him felt like pieces to a child's game. He seemed to win no matter where he went or what he did. Because of this, there was no emotional passion for anyone in Robert's life, especially for Daniela.

"How do you make a man into an assassin? I thought you said Payton was one of the best. And talent like that you have to born with."

"Born with, yes. But controlled, that is another thing. It's been a year since we took control of Payton, and now it's time for us to take back our country. Soon General Delgado will be El Presidente Delgado, and we will have our country back under our family's control," Robert said as he looked back at Daniela lying on the bed. Her red hair fanning the pillow.

"So all of these transactions, these exchanges, are to raise money for his campaign?" Daniela asked running her hand over her smooth stomach hoping to catch his eye.

"Soon there will be no competition, and the people will be free to elect their only choice," Robert said focusing once more on the scene below his tenth story window.

"What's to keep the people from finding out the election was won by default?"

"Here in the states people spend millions of dollars on smear campaigns to get rid of the competition. In El Salvador, we just get rid of the competition," Robert said with a smile that made Daniela shiver.

"Is that where Payton comes in? Is he your eliminator?"

"We have someone else taking care of that. Payton is here to kill me." Robert smiled a handsome, devilish grin.

"What do you mean? Here to kill you?" Alarm clearly visible on Daniela's face.

"I should say, Payton is here to kill my wife and make it look like she took her own after shooting me," Robert confessed.

"And what about your body? You can't have a murder-suicide without a body," Daniela said smugly.

"That is where Payton comes in. After he does his job, I will take him out, plant my identification on him, and burn that beach house to the ground." Robert continued to watch the scene below, his confession to Daniela as casual as a conversation about the weather.

"But I thought you said you were going to give the beach house to me?" Daniela whined as she pursed her lips out. Robert ignored her comment as he watched the activity of half a dozen police cars surround the vehicles that catered to his family's businesses—laundering cash. The scheduled exchange of the money for the uncut cocaine was now being stalled due to incompetence. This infuriated Robert. He shifted from his left foot to his right and inched closer to the dirty glass. He held the binoculars tighter in his grasp. He already knew the only suspect being detained on the street below and the reason for it: two hundred thousand dollars of uncut cocaine.

"It looks the deal is going south," Robert said through gritted teeth. He turned to yell at Daniela, "Put out that damn cigarette."

Daniela was up in bed taking a long, loud drags from the cigarette. At Robert's sharp demand, she wrapped her lips around the filter with an air of defiance and took a one extra-long drag before she snuffed it out. "I guess the funds for the El Presidente election will have to wait," she said sarcastically.

"Looks like the police have our boy, Richie," Robert said in a tone of voice intending to hurt and humiliate Daniela.

"Richie?" her voice cracked. Robert knew her love for her husband, Richie, was genuine, and what she had with him was just a deal. Robert was Richie's drug source from Central America. In exchange for Richie's safety, Daniela provided more than paralegal services to Robert, she was his whore.

Robert's attitude about Richie concerned Daniela, so she slipped out of the warm, king size bed into the light chill of the morning air. The cool air caused a chill to run up and down every curve of her sensual frame. As she stood, she pulled the top sheet with her and wrapped it around her model figure, creating a mock silhouette of a chiseled, white marble statue. Daniela walked towards Robert, before she reached him, she came to a standstill caused by the end of the sheet still snugly tucked under the end of the mattress. Reaching back and firmly grabbing the sheet, Daniela tugged it with no results. She continued to jerk it until the sheet pulled free, her actions caused the bed's comforter to fall to the floor. At the foot of the bed lay Daniela's red lace thong.

Daniela opened the sheet and wrapped her arms and the sheet around Robert's midsection. He felt the softness and the warmth of her firm breasts which momentarily distracted Robert from his focus.

"You know he will never turn on you, right?" Daniela said, trying to reassure Robert of Richie's loyalty.

Robert stared into Daniela's green eyes, "Does Richie know what you really do for me?"

"No. All he knows is that I'm your paralegal. You are the powerful District Attorney, are you not?" Daniela goaded.

"Do you know why we're so good together?" Robert asked as he pulled Daniela closer.

"Why's that, baby?" Daniela cooed into his ear.

"It's because in the dark, it's hard to tell when you are lying." A hint of a smile touched the corners of his lips just before he brushed them over her soft, full ones.

She pulled back. "That's the understatement of the year coming from one of L. A.'s top prosecutors, whose life as we know it is about to implode."

"I'm going to be just fine. You should be worried about our boy, Richie, down there," Robert said as he motioned with his head towards the street.

"You promised me you wouldn't hurt him. We had a deal. You made me a promise," Daniela begged.

His hand slid down to the small contours of her back as her hand came up to rub the firmness of his chest.

Daniela spoke in a sexy, raspy whisper, "You know I will do anything for you. Anything," she said as she met his cold grey eyes.

Daniela placed an open-mouth kiss on Robert's shoulder, nipping and then licking to sooth the bite. She continued to place kisses over his shoulder, down his arm, the sweat that still clung to his body from their recent sex left a bittersweet taste in her mouth. Daniela lifted her right leg and rubbed her inner thigh over Robert's leg, grinding her pelvis against him. He could feel the heat coming from her body. She wanted him, again, but only for Richie, always only for Richie.

"I know you want me," Daniela whispered as she trailed her fingertips over each sinew of his rock hard stomach. She continued south, running her hand down even lower. She could feel him already hard again.

"Come back to bed, my love, and let me take care of that for you."

≠

On the street below, Captain Montano had a bag of cocaine in one hand and a stack of $100 bills in the other. After rocking the weight of each back and forth in his hands, as if using the scales of justice, he handed the product and the paper over to one of his officers.

"Make sure all this gets logged into the evidence locker properly," he barked.

The fifty-something veteran cop, looking disturbingly like his bulldog, should have retired years ago. But with his children grown and his wife involved in more charity events than he could count, Javier Montano planned to remain a cop for as long as he could. But there were days like today when he didn't like his job. The corruptness, human callousness, and loss of life, like the dead body on the ground front of him right now. He watched as the ever changing blood pattern coursed over the sheet, absorbing the last of the suspect's restless soul.

≠

The rookie officer was only doing his duty when he drove up behind the tow truck that was assisting with what he thought was a driver with a flat tire. He parked his patrol car, with its lights on, at an angle to divert traffic, giving the tow-truck operator a little more room to work. Instead of appearing grateful, the officer observed the driver of the car and the tow truck driver were uneasy. Turning their bodies at odd angles to hide what they were doing. *"Why wasn't the tow truck driver changing out the flat using the owner's spare?"* thought the officer. He decided to run the plates on the car. They came back expired, and he immediately called for backup as a precaution.

When the second patrol car arrived, the suspect with the expired plates panicked and drew a weapon from the front seat of his car. In a matter of seconds, the Officers had taken the suspect down and the tow truck driver, Richie Finch, was in cuffs, asking for a lawyer.

As he was being frisked, Officer Taylor came across a crumpled scrap of paper which he removed from Richie's left, rear pocket. He gave the piece of paper to Montano. The barely legible writing on it: *216 Ocean*

*View, 7:15 Jag.* struck panic into the Captain. "Officer Taylor," Montano bellowed.

"Yes Sir."

"I want you get a hold of the D.A. I don't care if you have to bang on his bedroom door, just find him. Now."

"Yes, Captain. What am I supposed to tell him?" Taylor asked nervously.

"Tell him that we've come across some crucial information he needs to know about."

"Yes, Sir," Officer Taylor confirmed as he started to walk away.

"And Taylor?" Montano said firmly halting Taylor in his tracks.

"Yes, Sir," Officer Taylor said as he walked away.

"After you get a hold of him, take this evidence bag with the note in it and personally hand it to the lab boys. Wait there until they can tell you the name of everyone who has come in contact with it. I want it old news an hour ago."

Captain Montano flagged down another officer. "Officer Johnson."

"Yes, Sir," Johnson said running up to Montano.

"You and your partner need to transport our friend, Richie, to the station. Dump him in a holding cell and start cross checking the computer for the name Jag and Jaguar. Let me know what you come up with," Montano commanded.

"Yes, Sir."

Montano walked over to the tow truck and started helping the officers conduct the search of the few remaining spare tires that were strapped down in the back. It didn't take long before they found what all the drama was about. One of the tires held bags of cocaine and another held thousands of dollars in cash duct taped in large Ziploc bags.

"Holy shit," whistled one of the officers, "the mother lode."

"Exactly," said Montano. "But whose mother lode?"

≠

From his hotel room above the scene, Robert sat in a chair, talking on the phone. Across from him, Daniela was taunting him from the bed. She tied herself up by wrapping her wrists in the one end of the sheet, she placed the other end of the sheet over her eyes, then raised her arms over her head, as if being subdued and waiting to be taken. She listened to Robert's voice, but could not hear his words over the pounding of her own heart. She prayed what she was doing was enough to keep her husband, Richie, and herself alive for one more day. She arched her body, taunting him to come over to the bed. Anything to distract Robert from taking Richie out of the equation for the loss of his shipment.

"I need the work done tonight. The plans to the house and half the money will be at the new drop I just sent you. I've added substantially to your fee because I've decided I want you to take care of my wife, too," Robert informed Payton.

"The job was for one. I don't like last minute changes," asserted Payton.

Robert reached into a small duffel bag at his feet and pulled out a gun with a silencer. He slowly spun the two pieces of cold steel together forming them into one silent but deadly lethal weapon.

"It's an easy job for the amount of money I'm giving you. I want it to look like a murder-suicide. The distraught wife kills herself after killing her husband," Robert demanded.

Payton's voice was hesitant and suspicious; he didn't like plans changing at the last minute. "The job was to fake your death. Why are you adding your wife to the equation? Why not let her live long enough to keep Montano busy with the debriefing?"

"Because she's useless to me now. Can you fake my death, kill my wife, and put the blame of my apparent demise on her or not?" Robert barked into the receiver.

Payton didn't get paid to understand, to care, or to question. Yes, there were several times when he had to fulfill a contract despite his misgivings, but he had his reasons—Kate. As long as he did his job, Delgado would keep her alive. An assassin should be a machine, but Kate had his heart. He knew over the last year, Delgado had turned the only woman he loved into his own personal soldier, Delgado's Mia. Why was he even questioning killing this woman? He didn't know her. Killing her was just a means to an end and all Payton wanted was to get Kate back. The question was, would she still be the woman he loved?

"Where can I find her?" Payton asked.

# Chapter 6

Marisa picked up a couple of empty tin boxes along with her other items and put them in a towel. She tossed it over her shoulder hobo style while she slipped on her sandals, and headed home. Due to her injuries from a car accident few months earlier, Marisa walked cautiously, the uneven terrain emphasizing her slight limp. Each step was a painful reminder of a memory that had gone from elation to deflation.

Marisa was on her way home after dropping her parents off at the John Wayne Airport. They had come out for an awards gala honoring the exceptional work of photojournalists from the United States. Marisa had won an award in the category for the best photo that told a story without a caption. The photo was both horrific and mesmerizing.

It was of a local drug bust gone wrong. A raid by the police had been planned for a week. When they went to serve the warrants, someone had tipped off the gang and it had turned into to a blood bath. After all was said and done, the crime scene looked like a macabre painting.

In the background of the photo, was a white stucco building riddled with bullet holes. The front door was partially off its hinges. The officer who used a hand held battering ram on that door lay dead on the front porch steps, the battering ram still in his hand. Another officer lay on the steps leading to the front door, his right arm out-stretched, his gun in his hand. All of the building's windows were shattered from the exchange of bullet fire between the gunmen and the Santa Monica Police Department's Narcotics officers. Smoke billowed out of the house. Two ambulance personnel with a gurney stood behind a fire engine, clearly anxious to get to the downed officers.

The mid-ground angle of the photo had patrol cars on the left and right. On the car on the right, a dead officer laid spread eagle on top of the car's hood. To the left, an officer hid behind his squad car door. His bloodied left hand held his radio while his right arm rested on his thigh, the right hand nothing but a stub.

The emergency vehicle lighting of the squad cars had been heavily damaged. Most of the plastic was missing from one side exposing the whirling plastic cones. The sun's hot afternoon rays caused a flare to streak across a part of the picture.

In the near-ground, was the officer Marisa was standing behind as she raised her camera up over his shoulder and rattled off a series of shots in seconds. She knew it would be just a matter of time before she was asked to leave the crime scene, but it was enough to get the award winning shot. Marisa had earned the award all on her own. The thought crossed her mind that a few votes in her favor may have been influenced by the fact she was married to the District Attorney.

Robert had never taken her career seriously or ever given her credit or praise for her work. When guests came over to the house and saw Marisa's work hanging in the stairwell, Robert would dismiss their admiration with the comment, "What would you expect them to say?"

The more Robert referred to Marisa's passion as a hobby, the more it motivated her to get her own studio.

Marisa was able to recall most of the events of her terrible accident, but not all of them. Certain images and sounds created small panic attacks. She remembered the thumping sound of the brake pedal going to the floor, not once, but three times as she pumped harder and harder on the brakes. After that it was all in flashes of chaotic memories that were scrambled and came back in two second segments. The sounds of the tires squealing and hitting the center barrier then seeing the landscape through the windshield as the car rolled over and over. Then nothing for what seemed like an eternity as the car's momentum had taken flight before landing with brute force. Marisa's seat belt strap had ratcheted so hard that it popped her shoulder out of joint. The airbag released in the blink of an eye and hit her face with the force of a boxer's punch. The pain was so incredible she hadn't realized her leg was broken.

When the car finally stopped spinning upside down on its hood, Marisa tried to push the airbag away. The smell of smoke and gasoline filled her nostrils. The memories after that were flashes of panic, chaos and sirens. Panic had filled her entire being as she felt her feet getting hot. This meant the car engine was on fire. Marisa looked off to the side through the shattered driver's window and saw a trail of gasoline slowly running toward her. She knew she had to get out and that was when she realized her leg was broken and pinned under the dash.

For a full 60 seconds, Marisa felt what it was to be truly alive. Every part of her was conscious at the moment. That one brief amount of time that gave you such clarity you knew you wanted to live, not the life someone had planned for you, but your life. She thought at any moment she would be looking down on her own crash scene from above as if taking an aerial shot of her own accident, one that would be on the cover below the fold of tomorrow's paper with the headline, "D.A.'s wife who never had a life."

The blast from the fire extinguisher momentarily took her breath away. Extreme pain followed as the Sheriff's deputy tried to cut her free from the seat belt and get her out of the car. When they had to use the Jaws of Life to get her out, the strong ripping vibrations shook her leg so bad the pain caused her black out.

Marisa opened her eyes to find herself behind a curtain in the surgery recovery area of the Intensive Care Unit. She tried to move her arms without success. Taking inventory of her injuries, her right hand had hoses and wires attached, her left arm was in a sling after having had her shoulder re-set, and her left leg was in a cast almost up to her hip. A brace circled her neck and she could feel the gauze that was taped to left side of her face. Her IV must have some pretty good drugs because she wasn't feeling a thing except for her dry throat.

A doctor parted the curtain, followed by a nurse who held a small paper cup of chipped ice to help soothe her throat.

"Hello, Marisa. I'm Dr. Yoshino. I performed the surgery on you. How is your pain level?"

Marisa looked at the IV hanging up above her and smiled.

"I'm fine, Dr. Yoshino, thank you."

"You're going to be fine, Marisa," Dr. Yoshino assured her. "Your husband, Robert, is here. Shall I have the nurse bring him in?"

Marisa shook her head, no.

"Okay. First off, do you remember the accident?"

With a slight nod, Marisa confirmed his question.

"I don't have a full report but from what I can gather from the officer who was first on the scene, you somehow lost control of your vehicle and hit the center barrier. Apparently this caused your car to roll over. Your left leg was pinned under the dash and you suffered a clean break in the middle of your femur. Your left shoulder separated as well. You have a few minor cuts on the left side of your face."

Tears rolled down Marisa's face.

"You're going to be fine. When the airbag went off, it caught most off the glass. The bandages are just there to help the medicine to its job and keep your skin from scarring. In a few weeks, those minor cuts shall be all healed."

Marisa touched the brace around her neck.

Dr. Yoshino said gently, "I don't want you be scared, the neck brace was only a precaution, your x-rays came back negative on the neck area. I just didn't want you waking up and trying to get out of bed until the anesthesia wore off. Here, let me take that off of you." Dr. Yoshino carefully removed the collar.

Marisa took a deep breath of relief and in a raspy voice asked, "Have my parents been notified? They were on their way back up to Napa."

Dr. Yoshino motioned to the nurse who left the area for a minute and returned with a Sheriff's deputy. Yoshino gave the room to the officer.

"Hello, Mrs. Westmore. My name is Steve Sherwood."

"Are you the officer that saved me?"

"Yes, I am."

"Have you been able to reach my parents? Do you need their cell phone number?"

"I'm afraid there's been an accident. I was informed that the plane your father was flying went down about twenty minutes after take-off."

Marisa wanted to scream, but her raspy voice and heavy sedation only allowed her to cry.

"My parents?"

"I'm sorry. There were no survivors."

Marisa's worst fear had come true and she began to shake uncontrollably. The officer called the doctor. When Dr. Yoshino saw Marisa so agitated, he increased her sedation medication.

After a lengthy stay at the hospital and hours of therapy on her shoulder, Marisa was finally home.

Resting peacefully was not an option as her mind replayed the accident and devastating loss of her parents.

Robert had a queen size Craftmatic bed put in the den on the main level of their house. It faced the ocean to help Marisa to sleep and stay as comfortable as possible during her recovering. Most nights, Robert would make dinner when he got home. On the weekends, he would get a fire going in the fireplace and stay with Marisa in the bed downstairs.

When the cast finally came off, it was easier for Robert to pay for a physical therapist to come to the house twice a week than to shorten his work schedule to come all the way back to the house to take her.

After a couple of weeks, Marisa was able to use the stairs, but preferred to use the bed down stairs in the den. The ocean was her haven. She made it her goal to eventually be able to take long walks along the shore at noon and sunset without being winded. There was nothing like the feel of the wind in her hair and the sun on her face to take her mind off the accident. She wasn't so much concerned of her own accident, the police had told her the brakes had failed, it was a good thing her seat belt was on, and she hadn't been going any faster or she would have more than likely been thrown from the car and killed.

The only accident that was keeping her up at night was that of her father's plane going down. Her father had made that trip several times and was a fanatic about doing his own plane maintenance. He used to fly fisherman on trips all around Alaska until he retired a few years ago and that's when her parents decided to move to Napa. He flew a Cessna Skyhawk 172S he rebuilt with a buddy he had known since high school.

Her husband, Robert, had told her he didn't want to bother her with the details but he had seen the reports regarding both accidents: hers and her parents. Both had been exactly what they said, accidents and he would go over them when she was feeling up to it.

Today was different. Marisa went to the beach today to say goodbye. She took the two tin boxes that held her parents ashes off of the fireplace mantle and decided today was the day. She took a glass of wine with her down to beach to have one last toast to her parents before she ceremoniously tossed their ashes into the ocean.

She remembered her mother as a good cook and how she laughed each time she asked her mom how she made her spaghetti sauce so good. Her mom could never tell her. She always used to say, "I just throw in what's ever handy." It didn't matter; it was always the best because it was Mom's.

Marisa's father was the one who got her interested in photography. She remembered that every time he came back from his fishing tours. He would show her amazing pictures of the rivers and valleys. Best of all, she loved the stories that went with each photo. He used to tell her, "Don't waste your film. Make sure every picture tells a story." She never forgot that.

That's what Marisa was doing down there on the beach that day. Remembering.

# Chapter 7

Marisa was about to go up the back stairs when she heard some kids laughing as they ran up the shoreline being chased by a dog. She sat her items at the base of the stairs and walked over to the slider off the back porch, disappeared into the house for a minute then returned with her camera strapped around her neck. As she walked out the phone rang. She hesitated for a minute but she knew it just had to be Robert calling to check on her and she decided to let it ring.

With her father's words fresh on her mind, she wanted to take some pictures that really made her feel better about herself, and didn't want to disappoint him. She was still Daddy's little girl but had bloomed into a beautiful, grown woman. Her dad always said she could have been a model but Marisa was more comfortable behind the camera. He even gave her a loan to get through a photography school of her choice and all he asked was for her to pay back the loan when she could. When she started working freelance and got on with the L.A. Times, she was able to pay back the entire loan. That was one of the many things she loved about her parents. Even though Marisa was an only child, they never spoiled her, only encouraged her to do better.

A stiff salty breeze had come up and drew a bit of cool air in off the ocean. Marisa shifted her feet so the sun baked sand covered them like warm slippers. She steadied her arms close to her tall, lithe body as she focused her camera in on a dog running down the beach with a top to a woman's bikini in its mouth. A topless woman with her arms crossed over her breasts, yelled at a man as she left the ocean's surf. From what Marisa could hear, the half-clad lady was demanding the man get control of his dog and return her bikini top from where it had snatched it from her towel. Marisa clicked off a few shots then lowered the camera. The smile on her face was giving away her thoughts. Did this guy really teach his dog to fetch bikinis? Her next thought swiveled around to her own identity. Could she ever feel confident enough to swim half naked in public? Robert treated her like a centerpiece, an object to show off in his high profile lifestyle. For the first time in years, Marisa started thinking about what she thought about herself.

As the dog continued down the shoreline, Payton focused his camera on Marisa. Her smile absorbed all his attention. When her expression moved to one of distraction, he didn't remember capturing that smile. The click of the shutter was his only clue that he had used his camera. Marisa unsettled him. Maybe it was the fact that for once, he wasn't just looking at a target. He was feeling something he wasn't supposed to.

    As Marisa took in the beauty and charm of the Pacific Ocean, she noticed a man standing on a sand dune about a hundred yards away pointing a camera in her direction. She watched as his lens followed the dog as it ran on by. That's when Marisa lifted her camera to her face and pointed her high powered lens on him. She watched as he lowered his camera and took a call on his cell phone. She couldn't get a good look at him because of the aviator sunglasses he wore and a baseball cap. The man's physical build was impressive. Marisa's thoughts came across in her smile admitting to herself he looked pretty good in those faded jeans and that white long sleeve cotton shirt with its cuffs rolled up nicely just above the elbow. His shaggy hair whipped slightly from the wind from around the edges of his old baseball cap that had seen better days. Marisa watched as he continued to play in the sand with his foot like a nervous habit. She liked the view even better when he turned and walked away in the other direction.

Just for an instant, Marisa silently pleaded to the stranger, turn around and look back one more time. He did. That's when she rapidly ran off of three consecutive photos. She may not have captured his eyes behind those sunglasses, but he certainly captured her imagination. Marisa wondered if this was the first time he had been to her beach and if he would ever return.

The wind was starting to pick up and she had remembered Robert saying something about coming home early. It was Marisa's turn to choose what was for dinner and she decided on barbecued chicken, but first she wanted to marinade it so she headed for the house to get herself cleaned up before dinner.

Marisa was mildly winded as she walked up the wide steps to her home. The house was built in 1978 and looked worn on the outside. Inside, it was a decoration mixture of modern and antique. There were three bedrooms and two baths that had been recently remodeled to both Robert's and Marisa's tastes. The second bedroom wall had been removed to make the master bedroom a large sanctuary for the active couple. A 42 inch TV hung on the wall opposite the king size bed and a 24 inch one was mounted in the bathroom. All the TV's throughout the house doubled as monitors for the state of the art security system that ran through the house. The original small back to back closets had been combined into one large walk-in. The master bathroom was widened to make room for a walk-in shower. The shower walls were made of six inch cubed glass designed to cause a wavy appearance when looked through from the other side. A rain showerhead and side sprays completed the opulence. Off the master bedroom was a balcony where most mornings Robert and Marisa sat at a small, white café style table and drank coffee while admiring the gorgeous panoramic view of the Pacific Ocean.

    The real value of the couple's home though, was the private strip of beach in front of the house. It was far enough from the ocean so the pounding of the waves against the shore didn't sound like thunder, more like a hum from the earth's center.

    In their master bathroom, Marisa undressed and was ready to enter the shower when the phone rang. By the time she reached the phone it had gone to messages. She hit the playback code on her phone.

"Robert, its Daniela. We need to talk before tonight's final merger…call me."

The sound of seduction wrapped around the woman's words. After the initial shock of betrayal faded a small percentage, Marisa's anger filled the interior of the house. On her way back to the bathroom, she used the back of her hand to swat a picture of her and Robert off the shelf. It fell to the hardwood floor, the glass in the frame breaking into a hundred sharp pieces.

In the back of Marisa's mind this betrayal was something she suspected would one day happen. When she and Robert met, he had been attentive, kind, and generous to her. He was a handsome, successful District Attorney and Marisa was immediately enthralled with his charismatic personality. The courtship and engagement was brief, but both of them felt right for each other. But over the years, Robert changed. He became distant, short-tempered, and absent on a frequent basis. Marisa had confronted him on several occasions about a story she was working on and he had basically told her, "Let it go, you're not a real reporter."

Robert may have had some influence on Marisa getting the job as a photojournalist, but she was good at her profession. She knew how to frame each shot to be most effective in telling the story. The detectives who processed the crime scenes that worked with her, repeatedly told Marisa she was one of the best in her field.

Did the guys just tell her that because Robert was the District Attorney or was there the chance they really believed she had the talent for the job? She didn't care, she knew what she was doing was good work.

Marisa bent over and picked up the damaged photo off the floor. She felt a head rush come over her. Was it the anger she was feeling or something else. All she knew was she wanted to vomit. She had thrown up when she first got up this morning. Robert had asked her if she was okay and Marisa brushed it off as something she probably ate the night before.

The last two weeks had been crammed tight with appointments, negotiations, parties, fights with Robert and make-up sex.

"Pregnant?" The thought washed panic over Marisa and she nearly fell as she entered the shower. "Not now, please God, not now."

In Marisa's dream, she found herself running in all directions trying to find the source of a desperate cry. Robert was standing in the middle of the room and the closer she got to him, the louder the cry. Yet, when she asked her husband where the cry was coming from, his response was always, "What cry?"

The shrill of the phone woke Marisa from her nightmare. She had lain down on the bed for only a moment after her shower and had fallen into a deep sleep.

"Hello," her voice sounded thick and confused, like the dream now fading from her mind.

"Hello, Mrs. Westmore, this is Officer Taylor calling for Captain Montano. Could I speak to Mr. Westmore please?"

"He's not here. Can I take a message for him?"

"No, that's okay, Mrs. Westmore; we just need to ask him a few questions."

Marisa paused, shook her head in an attempt to clear it. "Did you try his office?"

"Yes, I've tried there already. They haven't seen him since this morning. Did he happen to mention his schedule for this afternoon?"

"No...Did you try his pager?"

"I'll try that next, thank you, Mrs. Westmore."

"You're welcome."

Marisa hung up the phone in disgust. She sat, then stood up and waited a few moments before taking small steps to make sure her legs were steady. After several minutes, she hit the redial button on the phone.

A familiar voice answered on the other end.

"Hello."

"Hello...Claire?"

Robert's mother Claire was in her early sixties. She had a strong, round body and handsome face. There was more bravado in her than most men. Marisa could hear the sounds of Claire's favorite pastime, baking. Metal cookie sheets banged against oven racks, the oven door being closed and the timer being set.

"Marisa honey, is that you? Are you alright?"

Marisa could barely hear over the ringing in her head. Everything in the room seemed to be absorbing all the ambient sounds and the tone of the ringing fading in and out with her breathing. It was all she could do not to think of Robert with another woman.

≠

Robert admired the soft pink and light blue hues of dusk while he talked to police dispatch.

"Yes, I'm waiting to be patched through to Montano. Thank you."

Montano was tired and hungry as he drove from the crime scene back to the station house. He shook his head in frustration as he heard dispatch announce his call number over the police radio.

"Come in thirty-two x eleven."

"X eleven, go ahead."

"The D.A. is waiting for you on channel two."

"Thank you, dispatch."

Montano switched channels on the radio.

"Go ahead, Robert."

"Javier, I think someone is trying to kill me."

"He's in line after me." Montano chuckled softly before returning to a professional tone of voice. "Does the name Jaguar mean anything to you?"

Montano's question was met with a combination of silence and airwaves crackling.

"Did you copy, Robert? I said, does the name Jaguar mean anything to you?

"No, should it?"

"I have something of interest for you. Can you meet me at the station in twenty minutes?"

"Twenty minutes sounds like a plan, I'll be there."

# Chapter 8

Robert stroked Daniela's ankle during his conversation with Montano. When the phone call ended, he placed another call. There was no acknowledgment from the person on the other end.

Robert said, "It's time."

After Robert hung up the phone, he removed the smoking silencer from his gun. Void of remorse, he stood next to the bed and watched as the blood from Daniela's dead body spread across the white sheet. He watched as the blood momentarily gave the illusion of a crimson rose blooming over her heart before the blood saturation changed the appearance altogether.

Daniela died instantly, two shots through the heart. The moment she saw Robert aim the gun at her she had only one thought; the promises that were made and the lies kept.

As Robert started removing evidence of his existence from the hotel room, his beeper went off. He didn't bother to look at the screen because this time it was a signal, not a message. A minute later, Robert went to the door and let two of his men in. They each put on surgical gloves and began to wipe down the room. In one of the wastebaskets, was an open condom wrapper. Using a glove, Robert picked it up then pulled the glove from his hand enveloping the wrapper inside the glove. He put it and Daniela's cigarette butt in the wastebasket liner and tied the bag shut; tossing it with other garbage bags containing proof of his crime. Robert reminded his guys to be thorough in cleaning the room, then left.

His gun already holstered, Robert put his jacket on and walked towards the hotel elevator. As the elevator doors opened, his cell phone rang; the caller I.D. showed it was his wife, Marisa. Robert let the call go to voice messaging.

In the den, Marisa sat at Robert's desk waiting for him to answer her call. Feeling a range of emotions she couldn't even begin to describe, Marisa opened a side drawer of the desk and saw a gun. She didn't bother to leave a voice message before she hung up the phone. As she removed the hand gun from the drawer, she reflected on the story of how Robert came home with the gun. He had said he brought it home for protection after a case had gone the other way and the suspect had got off on a technicality and wanted it just in case his work had followed him home. She hit the release button on the Beretta and watched the gun's clip fall free.

≠

Payton held his 9mm Beretta in his left hand and the clip in his right. He sent the clip home and made sure the silencer was snug. Pulling the slide back it cleared the existing round for a new one. In a well-worn shoulder harness beneath his black leather jacket, he put the pistol away then adjusted the strap of his digital camera around his neck. Payton's movements replicated the style and grace of a panther, smooth yet unpredictable. For a man of forty, he had seen the thousand ways humanity inflicts horror upon itself. His face and body displayed the numerous stories of being captured and beaten to the edge of death. Fortunately for Payton, his mind was strong and sharp. In his business he couldn't afford to let it get personal. He let his guard down once and it almost cost him his life and his love.

From his position on the balcony, Payton watched Marisa get undressed as she entered the bathroom. He waited until she turned on the shower so it would hide the sound of him picking the lock and the sliding glass door as he entered the room. Curious about his target, Payton observed what seemed to be Marisa's nightstand at the side of the bed. Besides a lamp, there is a small frame of her and her husband, Robert and a book titled, *"Guardian of the Red Butterfly."*

Just outside the bedroom, photos of Marisa hung on the wall. From the age of three until what looks like a fairly recent one, Payton noticed the same thing in every picture; a smile so captivating it nearly takes your breath away. He also learns from the photos that Marisa's maiden name was Alexander. Not sure how long he had been admiring Marisa's photos, Payton took a quick peek in the bathroom to make sure she was still in the shower, to his relief she was.

The glass cubes that made up the inner part of the surround were clear enough to make out the shape of Marisa's body, yet the view was slightly distorted. The outer wall window was also clear cubed except for a portion from two to four feet was frosted so anyone looking from outside the house would only see her legs from the knees down and her head above the frosted section of the glass. The glass wall also contained a lighting track on the inside that was controlled by a dimmer. Marisa had set it half way creating a nice glow that highlighted the steam from the shower.

Payton couldn't tell if she had turned her back to him so he shifted his weight to get a better look. Through the open passage into the shower, Payton could see Marisa's vivacious figure as she washed her arms and legs. He found himself at odds with his own morals. When Payton took the assignment, he didn't count on feelings he thought he had put away long time ago; that of caring for someone else. He was losing sight of his objective, his mission. There was something about her he had noticed the first time he saw her through the lens of his camera on the beach. The way she moved, her skin tone, the way her hair brushed across her shoulders, Marisa reminded him of Kate. He silently made his way to her closet, removed Marisa's full length silk bathrobe and laid it on the edge of the bed.

During Marisa's long warm shower she tried to make a mental list of all of the good times she and Robert had shared and realized there weren't any of her own. They all seem to paint a picture of standing in the background in Robert's shadow. The only time she felt in control was in the bedroom and even then it was to please him. That's what was missing in her life, pleasure. She had become a slave to his urges and not his lover. She had lost her own identity. As Marisa leaned against the shower wall she felt the weight of the moment and let herself slide down the wall. She sat on the floor looking up at the water coming down on her like rain, wishing it could wash away the pain in her heart.

Payton took one long last look at this beautiful woman who had no idea that her husband had planned for today to be her last. He closed his eyes as if to say a prayer and asked God for an answer. But after what happened in El Salvador, Payton had questioned his own faith. When he had agreed to work for Delgado in order to save Kate, his personal convictions changed. He had left Kate with a madman. Payton's shame turned to anger. As Payton started to walk away, Marisa looked up in his direction. She saw nothing, but still felt intrusion within herself.

Stepping out of shower, Marisa dried then wrapped herself in a soft thick Egyptian towel. She used her hand to wipe steam off the bathroom mirror. The woman staring back at her seemed like a stranger.

As Marisa entered the bedroom, she immediately noticed her silk robe draped across the end of the bed. She knew Robert wasn't due home for a few hours. Had she pulled it out herself and just forgot? All day her mind had been wondering so it was completely possible she had forgotten this small everyday occurrence.

She turned to face the hallway. "Hello, Robert. Are you home?" Marisa repeated as she walked into the main living area of the house. Only silence greeted her as she called out and looked for evidence of someone else in the house.

Not getting a reply, she returned to the bedroom. Between the phone message, the conversation with Claire, the possibility of pregnancy and the divorce decision; it's no wonder she didn't remember what she did and didn't do. Marisa dropped her towel and put on the robe, she was about to leave the bedroom when a breeze squeezed itself through the tiny opening of the balcony sliding glass door. Marisa may have lost her mind but she knew one thing—she would have never left the back door open while she showered. Quietly and cautiously she looked out the sliding glass door and saw a small object sitting on the balcony table. Upon closer inspection, Marisa gasped when she realized it was a fully intact bullet.

≠

Robert drove his stylish and plush black car into the space marked "RESERVED D.A." He reached into the glove box and pulled out his ID badge then slapped the glove box lid closed. The car's insignia, a Jaguar, cast a ghoulish shadow in the harsh parking garage lights.

Inside Robert's office, he and Montano discussed strategy concerning Robert's death threats.

"When you said someone was trying to kill you I thought you were joking. Now you're telling me you think it's going down tonight and you're fine with this idea of playing right into his hands?" Montano shoved the last of a stale bologna sandwich in mouth, an action designed to give him a few more moments to think about the impending situation.

Robert withheld a look of disgust as he watched his friend eat like a starving hyena. He returned to cleaning his already clean fingernails with a pocketknife, "You've done this kind of operation plenty of times, Javier."

"But not with you as the bait. Do you really trust your source? I want to talk to this guy of yours."

"There isn't enough time to make it happen. Trust me, Javier, have I ever steered you wrong?"

There were plenty of times when Robert was wrong, but Montano wasn't about to tell the District Attorney that, even if they were friends. "Speaking of time, Robert, two minutes down the road is too far."

Robert's laugh was slight as he said, "I'll be alright, besides any closer and you'd be spotted."

"You just make damn sure you hit that transmitter in time. If he spots it, you're dead."

"That's the idea." Robert rapped on his chest with his fist making a hard thumping sound against the bullet proof vest.

"This is no game, Robert, and this guy is no amateur. He has the address to your new house and you've only had it a few weeks."

"You mentioned the name, Jaguar. Where did that name come from?"

"During the bust, one of my guys found a perp holding a slip of paper with the name 'Jag' on it. We're cross checking the files for similars. So far all we get is Jaguar. The computer hasn't come up with anything else so far; hence, we have a new player."

"Jaguar? I like it. It will look good in bold type in a headline."

"Either this guy has beginner's luck or he's an old face with a new name. I'm betting the latter."

"And what, my friend, makes you think that?"

Montano handed Robert a file. "This is why. It's my new pet project. It may be thin but it's really juicy where it counts. Between the lines, if you know what I mean. I already feel as if I know this guy, but...I get so...so…" Montano sighed as his massive hands rubbed his face. "Pissed off! We get decent leads just to see them go bust. This guy's just like a greased pig. I'm so close, Robert."

"Calm down, my friend, you're going to give yourself a heart attack."

Montano grabbed his blood pressure pills from out of his pocket as Robert handed him a glass of water from the cooler. The flush-faced cop took the pills and swallowed the glass of water in one gulp.

Slightly breathless, Montano said, "I really want this guy."

"I know, Javier, let me take the file home and study it while we're waiting for this Jaguar fella to show himself tonight."

"I'm not sure about this whole thing, Robert. The risk factor is off the scale."

"Java, my man, not to worry, I'm hard wired this time. Plus, I have this transmitter, press it, and you're there in two minutes." Robert held a hand size transmitter in his hand and pressed the button. On the laptop between them, the device had a program running to record and the light flashed as the program and started to record.

"And if the wire goes out, Robert?"

"Give me five minutes."

"Let's recap. You come to me with an attempt on your life story that involves not telling your wife, risking your own life in the process, and you want me to play along because..."

"Because I know you will be there when I need you, Javier."

"We have an unknown factor in play here...What if Marisa walks in, then what?"

# Chapter 9

The Pacific Coast Highway at night was a maze of head lights and tail lights that serpentined up and down the once desert shoreline. A skyline of muted mauve colors highlighted silhouettes of palm trees and seagulls riding along the warm coastal breeze.

Everyone seemed to be in a hurry to make it home in time for dinner or to rush to a party they thought couldn't start until they arrived. Now they had to wait just a bit longer as an ambulance running a code 2 with red and blue lights whirling and no siren tried to get through the traffic jam.

The plan was too complex for Captain Montano's taste. Too many variables and not the least of which was Marisa. Montano's police issued squad car was pacing behind the ambulance and behind him was Westmore in his Cadillac Escalade. Montano hit the speed dial on his cell phone as his car's system takes over the call.

"Yes?" Westmore's voice was its usual cool tone.

Montano's concern was from his heart, "Remember, you only have two minutes."

"And five if I lose the wire," Westmore's reply revealed his lack of concern.

"And none if he shoots you in the head. You know we should have let Marisa in on this scheme of yours."

"Marisa is the least of our worries."

Westmore hung up the phone as they turned on a side street just around the corner from his house. All three vehicles parked in a corner lot about a mile up the road.

Westmore had parked his car facing the opposite direction of Montano's so the driver's doors were side by side. They each lowered their driver side windows.

"I still don't feel right about this. We need to find out more about this new player, this Jaguar. We may be jumping the gun a too soon."

"That's exactly why we're doing this. We get the shooter in the act, we flip him, and we get the Jaguar. Then you can retire a happy man knowing I owe you one for saving my life."

Before Montano can reply, Westmore gave him the thumbs up, and drove away.

≠

The handle on the inside deadbolt on the front door of the Westmore home silently turned, followed by the door handle, then with a slight push, the door slowly opened. The interior entry light was off. As the door opened, a dark figure of a man created from the porch light, cautiously entered the house. The figure slipped inside the doorway and quietly closed the door behind him. At first, the house appeared to be empty as the only sound heard were the chimes of the grandfather clock striking on the quarter hour. When the clock was silent, a slight slapping of the waves could be heard as they crashed on the distant beach. From down the hallway, classical music was drifting out from the den; someone had just turned on the stereo in Westmore's office.

Marisa emerged from the den and headed towards the kitchen without noticing the man that stood just inside the front door. She took out of the refrigerator a whole chicken and fresh asparagus for dinner. At the kitchen sink, Marisa rinsed the food with cold water from the faucet. The sound of the water was enough to mask the steps of the figure as he slipped passed the archway down the hall and into the den.

Robert went to the wall unit in the den and took out a small video camera and inserted a new flash card. He pushed the camera record button and then placed it in the corner of the bookshelf in order to get full coverage of the room.

As Robert unlocked the sliding glass door he saw a shadow reflected in the glass. He turned expecting to see Marisa, but instead was greeted by Payton.

Payton put one finger to his lips as his other hand holding a gun, motioned Robert to have a seat behind his desk. There was no mistaking the meaning when Payton leveled his Beretta at Robert's mid-section. Robert tried to hide the panic button in his hand, but Payton noticed every subtle move he made. Payton held out his hand towards Robert as an indication that he should hand over the device. After he handed over the mechanism to Payton, Robert took a seat at his desk with his hands in plain sight on top of the desk while the killer he hired held him at gun point. Payton again motioned with one finger to his lips for Robert to be quiet then points to his chest and whispers, "The wire." Robert reached down to the small of his back and unplugged the wire from its power source.

A mile down the road in a vacant lot, Montano heard a popping sound from the recorder program on his laptop go quiet. He reached for the ignition, but before he could start the car the machine popped again.

Marisa's voice came in loud and clear. "I said, move away from my husband."

Montano cringed and reached for the ignition once again, then stopped. Reached and then stopped again. He looked to the laptop for a clue of what to do next.

Robert's hand was still on the plug where he had just plugged the wire back in. He didn't move except to look at his wife Marisa, who was standing in the doorway holding a gun.

Marisa reiterated her request, "I said, put the gun down and move away from my husband."

Payton stood motionless. Both men couldn't believe their eyes. This beautiful woman in her bath robe has them both, dead to rights. Payton finally nodded his head and moved away from the desk, but kept his gun aimed in Robert's direction. Both men noticed that Marisa also had her gun pointed in Robert's direction. Marisa slowly lowered her gun off of Robert. Payton did the same, lowering his gun away from Robert as well. Both men noticed Marisa's hand was shaking.

Payton calmly said, "Put the gun down. You're not going to kill anyone. If you were, you would have done it by now."

Robert continued to play the victim, "Marisa, what are you doing?"

Payton raised his gun back on Robert.

Payton and Marisa simultaneously let Robert know exactly what they expected out of him. "Shut up!"

Upon hearing Payton bark out the same orders to her husband, Marisa's initial response was to point her gun at Payton. But then she realized Payton was already pointing his gun at her. Marisa thought about it for a moment and slowly raised her gun at Payton.

Marisa gave Payton the same response, "If you were going to shoot me, you would have already done it by now."

While Marisa and Payton were having their coup d'état, Robert had been slowly searching in the top drawer of his desk for his own gun. It was at that moment he realized two things: the gun Marisa was holding was his and Montano told Marisa the plan. The stereo in the room was still playing classical music. The haunting melodies were getting to Robert. His thoughts began to wander and then turn to panic when he realized his plan was no longer his plan. The anger he was feeling got the best of him and as he slowly tried to remove his hand from the drawer; his cufflink caught on the edge and rattled the drawer.

Without hesitation Payton turned and shot Robert in the chest sending him over backwards in his chair to the floor. Robert's pager was knocked loose from his belt and ricocheted under the desk.

Marisa was still holding her gun on Payton. "I may not be able to shoot my husband but I can certainly take a shot at killing you."

Payton laid his gun down on the edge of the desk still within arm's reach.

With an acid tone in her voice Marisa said, "You've done what you came here to do, now go."

"Aren't you curious who sent me here and why?"

"Okay, who?"

Payton pointed to Robert's body stretched out on the floor. "He did."

"Why?"

"I got paid to do a job."

"Well, I guess your job is done."

"Not quite, I need the file he kept in his safe."

"I don't know the combination to his safe so I guess it's time for you to go."

Marisa aimed at Payton's chest; he hit the transmitter on the panic button that was still in his hand. Sirens immediately began to wail in the distance. Marisa looked over her shoulder in the direction of the front of the house. She began to say something to Payton, but then realized he was already gone. The sliding glass door was open as Marisa cautiously made her way to the back door. The closer she got to the door, the more her heart pounded and the adrenaline coursed through her veins. Suddenly Marisa's senses were amped up. She could feel the swirling currents of the warm summer breeze and taste the ocean salt, strong and bitter, that it carried. As she reached the doorway she turned on the light switch next to the door and turned off the interior lights to the den. The full moon was on the rise and bright enough to light up the coastline. Marisa held the gun out in front of her and could see its silhouette against the ambient light of the moon. From the doorway Marisa looked out on the balcony and saw no one. The police cars with their deafening sirens arrived at the house. Marisa's heartbeat pounded so loud in her chest, she barely heard the sirens.

Montano was on the radio just a block away from the house. "I said, shots fired, at 2-1-6 Ocean View, man down, ambulance is already headed to the scene." Montano's car pulled into the driveway. He cut the sirens and right behind him, the ambulance.

In the den, Marisa had the safe open and was looking at a stack of saving bonds, some cash, and the file. She closed the safe quickly as she heard Montano pounding at the front door. Montano was about to kick the door in when Marisa turned the deadbolt and opened the door. The Captain and his men entered the house with guns drawn.

"Marisa, where is Robert?"

"He's in the den. He's been shot. A man shot him and he went out the back door."

Montano rushed down the hall followed by the EMTs. Marisa entered the den as the EMTs were already working on Robert. Marisa tried to get closer to her husband, but Montano took her by the arm and pulled her back out of the way.

"Let the EMTs do their job, Marisa."

"Is he dead?"

One of the paramedics turned to Montano as he pulled off his gloves, "Captain..."

Montano interrupted him, "I know. Cover the body and get him out of here, quickly."

Two uniformed cops, Stevens and Morris, entered the den.

Montano grabbed Marisa by the shoulders and tried to get her to focus, "Marisa, what did the man look like?"

Marisa's words fell slowly, "He was tall, dark hair, and had a gun. I really didn't get a good look at him."

Montano quickly began to bark out orders, "Stevens, take the beach and Morris, you take the front. He's close, find him."

The Paramedics quickly rolled Robert's lifeless body out on the gurney as Marisa tried to follow. Montano grip was firm, but gentle as he held her back.

"Robert! Javier, why is this happening?"

"Marisa, I need you to tell me more about this man who shot Robert. Can you do that for me? Come on, Marisa, keep it together."

Officer Stevens entered the den. "Not a trace of him, Captain."

Montano was trying to keep it together for the both of them, "Marisa, look at me. I need to know what Robert did with the file."

"He was sitting at his desk when I came in and interrupted the burglar. It must still be in the safe."

"Can you open it?"

"I don't know the combination. He had it changed recently."

Marisa pushed herself away from Montano's arms and ran out the front door to see the ambulance driving away. Marisa covered her ears as the sirens cut through the night air. Montano joined Marisa out at the curb. "I'm sorry, Marisa. Robert assured me he had this under control."

As Marisa turned back and looked at her friend, all Javier could see was the pain in her eyes.

The ambulance was just a few hundred yards down the road, still in range of the house, when the sirens went silent. Marisa collapsed into Montano's arms.

# Chapter 10

Robert Westmore's body was stretched out on the gurney in the back of the ambulance. The two paramedics just stared at the stillness at which his body laid there and they didn't bother to administer any medical assistance. They didn't need to.

"Are you all right, sir?" One of the paramedics asked.

"No," Robert mumbled with a slight ache in his voice. "That hurt like a son-of-a-bitch."

Robert tried on his own, but the pain was intense so the second paramedic helped him to sit up. Robert stuck his finger in the hole that was in center of his shirt where the bullet entered then lodged in his Kevlar vest. Trying out his best impression of Superman, Robert ripped open his shirt and to see what was left of his vest. The bullet had impacted and mushroomed just to the left of his heart. Robert reached for the Velcro on the vest but he was too sore and stiff to pull the strap. "Somebody help me with this damn thing."

Each of the paramedics pulled on the Velcro strips and carefully lifted the Kevlar vest off of Robert and tossed it to the floor.

≠

Montano walked Marisa back to the house as he consoled her.

"Javier! Is he dead?" Marisa's voice broke.

"Marisa, listen to me. Everything is going to be alright. I need you to be strong for me right now."

"Javier?"

"He's going to need your help to pull himself thru this."

Montano helped Marisa into the house. Her tears kept stride with her nervous pacing. Montano's words did little to comfort her.

"Robert and I have everything covered. That's why we had the ambulance waiting down the block."

For Marisa, the mere mention of Robert's name made her sick. She stopped long enough to give Javier a look that could kill then began to pace once more.

Montano tried to explain, "This whole plan was Robert's idea to draw out the man we think was hired to kill him. He didn't want to tell you and make you worry just in case it was nothing."

"Nothing? You call what happened tonight, nothing? My husband's been shot and as far as we know has died on the way to the hospital."

"Like I said, we've taken every precaution and he's going to be fine. Before you know it the phones going to ring and he's going to be asking for you. In the meantime, what can I get you Marisa, what do you need?"

"I need my husband, but I believe he needs someone else even more."

"What's that supposed to mean?"

"You're his best friend, Javier, aren't you? Now you're telling me you didn't know? What about the fishing trips to Baja? I guess you just talked about fish the whole time."

"We haven't been to Baja in months. I'm sorry, Marisa, I really don't know what you are talking about."

"If it's not you or me, then who is he spending his time with? Talk to me, Javier, what's going on?"

"There is no one else, I am sure of it. I'll tell you what, you wait here by the phone, and I'll call you when I have something solid for you. Okay?"

"Whatever."

Marisa began to twist and turn in agony. Her legs wanted to give way and so she took a seat on the steps at the bottom of the staircase. In doing so, the gun had begun to slide out of the pocket of her robe and onto her lap. Marisa hid the gun between her legs out of sight from Montano.

"Marisa, you look like you could use some rest. Let me help you up the stairs."

"No." She knew if she moved at all the gun would fall. "I just want to sit here for a minute. I'll be fine. I just need to catch my breath."

"I'm going to have one of my officers posted in the front and one in the back of the house for the night. You should be safe as long as you stay inside and away from the windows. If you need anything, anything at all, you let the officers know and they will help you."

The gun between Marisa's legs had begun to slowly slide down. Unable to stop it, she let it continue to slide down to the step below. She made small talk so any noise from its landing on the step might be covered up. The gun rested on the carpeted step so Marisa let her robe loosen a bit so it would fall a bit more to one side and cover it up.

Montano's concern was genuine, "Are you sure you are going to be alright? Would you like me to call someone to come stay with you, a friend perhaps?"

"I really would just like to be alone right now. Thank you, Javier."

"Okay, but if you need anything, you call me."

"I will. Thank you. Goodnight."

After Montano left, closing the door behind him, Marisa picked up the gun and looked at it for a moment. She noticed it was the exact same type gun the intruder had. It's a Beretta. Its black non-reflective surface was seductive and powerful at the same time. Marisa hit the clip release button and it came free into her other hand. She studied the bullets and how they stacked uniformly in the clip. Holding the clip in her palm, she used her thumb to wedge out a single round. Pinching the bullet between her fingertips, she studied how the light refracted off the bullet's brass casing. After a moment, Marisa placed the clip securely back into the gun and the gun back into the pocket of her robe. As she walked down the hall towards the den, Marisa rubbed the bullet between her fingertips like a lucky rabbit's foot.

Marisa entered the den and headed directly to the safe. She had once seen Robert dial the first and second numbers of the combination before as he tried used his body to block her view. She didn't need to see the third number to realize the combination to the safe was the day he had passed his bar exam to become a lawyer.

Marisa opened the safe, took out a file and began to read it. As she tried to comprehend what she was reading, Marisa took a look around Robert's office and spotted the small camera barely concealed on the bookcase. Rising from the desk chair, Marisa went over to the camera, hit the rewind for a minute and then play. On the small screen was the moment where Robert was going backwards when he was shot by Payton in the chest. As Robert's body fell to the ground, Marisa noticed something fall from his hip and ricochet off a nearby cabinet before coming to rest under the desk. Marisa stopped the recording. She pushed the desk chair back out of the way and realized, there was no blood. Not a single drop anywhere on the floor. She dropped to her knees, reached under the desk, and pulled out her husband's pager.

≠

Montano had rendezvoused with the ambulance back at the empty corner lot.

As he drove up, he saw his friend, Robert, sitting on the back bumper waiting for him. Montano pulled his car up next to the ambulance. Robert didn't say a word, walked around the car, opened the door, and took a seat on the passenger side.

"Where do you want to stay for the night?" Montano asked.

"How about the Embassy Suites?"

"Motel Six it is, and guess what, I already have a room booked for you."

Montano walked up to Delgado and handed him the keys to the room. "All they had was the penthouse."

Both Javier and Robert laughed. Montano then got serious.

"What about Marisa and the press?"

"What about 'em?" Robert's voice was cold and distant.

Montano didn't like his tone and Robert knew his quip was a slip of the tongue so he tried to cover it up. "We talked about this. We need to keep this under wraps or the whole thing can come back on the both of us."

Robert used the swipe key and entered the room followed by Montano.

"Gee, thanks for spending the entire budget on my room."

"Yeah, well at least you have a bed. If I don't get home soon, Kelly is going to have me locked out of the house, and then I'll have to come back here and bunk with you."

"Sorry, you're not my type."

"What is your type? Marisa told me about our fishing trip. How did we do? Did we have a good time? I hope it was worth it."

Westmore didn't answer.

"What's going on here, Robert? Is this some sort of seven year itch kinda thing?"

"There is no one else." Robert lied through his teeth and Javier knew it.

"I'm going to talk to the press in the morning then go check on Marisa. We need to tell her what's going on and soon. Not telling her could be putting her life in jeopardy."

Westmore turned his back on his friend. Montano stood in the doorway and waited for an answer. Robert finally responded to Montano.

"Yeah, tomorrow."

Montano again didn't like the aloofness in his friend as he closed the door behind him.

$$\neq$$

As Marisa walked up the staircase, she stopped by one of her pictures which lined the staircase wall. The pictures that were displayed were award winning photos of her as a crime scene photojournalist under her maiden name of Marisa Alexander. She made a small adjustment to one of them to correct its alignment. As she continued up the staircase, her eyes lingered over other photos she had taken over the years. Marisa's favorites were a set of photos of the coastline during a series of sunsets. As she reached the top of the stairs, a group of pictures of her more expressive nature, erotic and sensual photos were displayed.

Marisa entered her bedroom and stopped just inside the door, something wasn't right. She looked at the closet door. It was slightly ajar. Marisa slowly walked across the room and opened it. At first glance it looked undisturbed; but Marisa's gut told her something wasn't right. She cautiously parted some of her clothes and looked behind them, nothing. Then she noticed her hand was coated with a white chalky substance. The shoulder of her pink terry cloth robe also had the powder on it. Marisa looked up inside the closet and noticed the hatch leading to the attic. Chills filled her body with the thought that the man who shot her husband, probably didn't have time to run from the house and was now hiding above her.

All of Marisa's senses were now on high alert and she held back the sound of her own voice as she mouthed the words, "Oh my god." She slowly walked backwards while reaching into her robe pocket to pull out the gun. Not very long ago, Marisa knew she was not capable of killing anyone. Now, for the first time, the thought of actually having to kill someone crossed her mind.

Confused, she walked over to a chair that sat in a nearby shadow filled corner. She sat in the dark and listened to every little noise that the house made waiting for the unknown.

# Chapter 11

Marisa was still sitting upright in the chair she had fallen asleep in. She was tired from staying awake most of the night thinking about Payton; wondering if he was actually in the attic. It was unlikely he was able to go anywhere else. The police arrived so fast they would have seen him running down the beach. The last thing she remembered was looking outside from her second floor balcony and noticing the absence of fresh foot prints in the sand. From the bottom on the stairs to the ocean shoreline, anyone who had tried to make their way down to the beach would have left some sort of sign.

A loud thumping sound woke Marisa. It took a few moments for her to figure out where the knocking was coming from; the front door. Then the front doorbell rang. Her heart started to race, because if she heard it then surely Payton would have, that is, if he was still in the house.

Marisa tried to stand, but her right leg had fallen asleep. She tried to walk, but she could barely feel her foot on the floor and she fell to one knee.

The doorbell was ringing at a furious pace.

"I'm coming!" Marisa yelled.

She caught herself staring up into the closet. If he was up there, he had to know Marisa was now on the move. Lying on the floor in front of her was the pager. It had fallen off of her robe when she hit the floor. She picked up the pager and clipped it back on to the pocket on her robe. She felt for the gun in her pocket, it wasn't there. Panic closed her throat until Marisa realized the gun was resting on the side of the chair she had just stood up from. The doorbell rang again.

"Just a minute!"

Marisa was frustrated when she opened to door. It was Montano.

"Javier..."

"What took you so long to answer the door? I was just about ready to break it down."

"I was sleeping."

Montano quickly entered the house brushing past Marisa. He walked through the entry way and headed for the den.

"Is Robert here?"

"Isn't he at the hospital?"

"We didn't quite make it to the hospital. That's why I'm here. We have to talk."

Marisa looked up the staircase in the direction of her bedroom.

≠

Officer Stevens was walking the shoreline behind the house. From his position, he was able to see the light go on in the family room through the two large sliding glass doors as Montano and Marisa entered. He watched them pace back and forth through the room.

Inside, Montano had so many scenarios running through his mind he didn't know where to begin.

"What's going on, Javier?" Marisa had to make a decision, tell Montano about Payton possibly still being in the house or wait and see what Javier might say about the events from last night. "I think..."

Montano was in such deep thought her never heard Marisa. "Robert's involved..."

"With another woman, I know."

"It's not that. I mean...I think he's involved in something more. It's really involved, complex."

"Does it have to do with the case he is working on?"

"All I know is, he told me he has had threats on his life and he didn't want you to worry."

"What kind of threats, Javier? Where is he?"

"I don't know, but I can tell you he's not dead."

"He's not at the hospital and he's not dead. Where did you take him?"

Montano stops pacing. "Motel Six."

"Oh. I hear they have a really good care facility there."

Montano had worked himself into a frenzy over what he could and could not tell Marisa without putting her in danger. He began to sweat profusely and his throat became dry. "Can I have a glass of water?"

Marisa walked over to the wet bar and poured herself and Javier a glass of water.

"Here," Marisa handed Javier the glass of water and he drank half of it in one gulp. "Now tell me what is going on."

Marisa took a seat on the couch and waited for Javier to finish downing the other half of the glass.

Montano was now a little breathless. "Marisa, have you heard Robert mention the name, Jaguar?"

Suddenly the glass in Montano's left hand shattered. With his right hand he began to reach for his heart. The way her friend Javier was acting, Marisa thought he was having a heart attack. Montano took one step towards Marisa with a look of pure anguish on his face. One more step then he stumbled into Marisa's arms, dead. Marisa was practically crushed by the weight of the large man.

Marisa wrapped her arms around his chest and rolled Javier's upper body off to one side, enough so she could catch her breath.

"Javier?"

Marisa then noticed the blood on her hands. She was wrong about her friend, it wasn't a heart attack. He had been shot from behind just below the left shoulder blade. Before she could react, Marisa saw the sliding glass door open and a woman enter. She was dressed in black fatigues with a thin utility belt completely fitted with extra clips for her Beretta.

The woman stared at Marisa with the cold calculated look of vengeance in her eyes. She then turned and looked at the small bullet hole that had pierced the sliding glass door without shattering it.

"Sorry about the door." The woman raised her gun and pointed it at Marisa.

"Sorry about the robe."

Marisa shielded her face with her blood stained hands. She was shaking and felt the blood run down her arms. "Why are you doing this?"

"I wasn't here to kill him. He just got in the way." The woman walked over to Montano's body, grabbed him by the collar, and pulled him off of Marisa and let his body fall to the floor. She then grabbed Marisa by the front of her robe just below her cleavage and pulled her up to her feet.

"You just might live a little longer if you don't make me look for the file."

"What file are you talking about?" Marisa knew it was her only bargaining chip to stay alive.

"You don't want to play the type of games I play. Maybe, just maybe, I won't have to put a hole through this robe after all." The mysterious women pulled the robe off of Marisa's shoulder and saw a small tattoo of a bird in flight. "I just wanted to make sure I was talking to the right person. Marisa, right?" The woman smiled, an indication this situation was just a game to her.

"Who are you and why are you doing this? What did I do?"

"My name really doesn't matter but it's Mia. What does matter is you couldn't keep your nose out of the family business. I'm here because apparently someone can't fulfill the contract and thinks you're worth more alive than dead."

Marisa saw movement over Mia's shoulder, it was Payton lurking in the shadows of the darkened hallway. It was just a glance but what stood out was his steely eyes. So sharp, so focused.

Mia didn't miss the brief movement in Marisa's eyes. She knew her instincts were right, someone else was there. Payton knew he was made and with one fluid motion brought up his weapon and aimed it at Mia. Mia whirled and as she did, she exposed enough of her chest area to Payton to give him the opportunity to fire. Without hesitation they both fired their silenced Beretta's. Payton happen to get his off first, the bullet caught Mia in the chest. It sent her shot off target while his shot caught the center mass of her vest and slammed her to the ground. As Mia hit the floor, she dropped her gun which slid just out of reach.

Payton reached out this hand to Marisa, "Come with me, now."

"No..." Marisa instinctively replied.

Mia sat up, breathing heavy. "What's it been, Payton, just over a year? I see you decided to cut your losses."

Mia pulled back the material on her shirt to expose the light weight bullet proof Kevlar vest. Payton didn't miss his mark. If he wanted her dead, he would have taken the head shot. He knew Mia would be wearing the vest and knew why she was there. Delgado was playing his ace, Mia. Sending her to get to take out Payton and sending him a message that he still owned her.

Marisa started to move toward Payton but Mia grabbed her wrist. Mia used Marisa as leverage to stand. Payton aimed his gun at Mia once more. "Don't make me do this. Don't make me choose."

Mia's smile was not the same one Payton remembered and the look she gave him broke his heart; she was no longer his Kate. Over the last year, Delgado had turned her into the weapon of his own design.

Payton fired a second time and hit Mia center mass, but this time the bullet skipped across the face of her vest and grazed her left shoulder. Marisa was close enough to feel a light spray of Mia's blood splash across her face. Mia quickly gained control and pulled Marisa in front of her and used her as a shield. With her right hand Mia pulled up an Uzi on its swing shoulder harness from under her jacket. She put the Uzi to Marisa's ribs with authority.

Mia twisted the verbal knife. "So you couldn't just do what was asked of you?"

"That's all I've been doing and it's kept you alive," Payton said.

"I can see why you couldn't pull the trigger, Payton; she's a looker."

"That's not the reason and you know it."

Mia hadn't seen it at first, but now she did. She and Marisa had similar body types and hair color.

"Is this why you're defending Marisa, because she reminds you of me?"

Payton skirted the issue, not wanting to address an issue he hadn't fully figured out himself. "Let her go. She's coming with me," he demanded.

"No, I don't think so. I'm here to get the file and I need her to get it for me."

Mia maneuvered herself closer to the sliding glass doors as she continued to use Marisa as a shield. "This is for immunity and to make it through to the next round, Marisa. Where's the file?"

Payton interrupted, "Don't tell her. If you do, she'll kill us both."

Marisa knew Payton was telling the truth and her only chance was to deny she knew the code to the safe. "It is my husband's safe and the only way I am getting the combination is through our lawyer during the reading of his will."

Mia squeezed Marisa tighter and whispered into her ear. "Your husband, Robert, was like family, so I will give you twenty-four hours to come up with the combination of that safe or the next time we meet, it's not going to end well for you." Mia spoke louder so Payton could hear. "You see, Payton and I have a very special bond, we were once a team. We depended on each other." Mia gave Marisa little extra jab to remind her of the gun in her ribs.

Payton knew he needed to get back the momentum. "Let Delgado know I will get him the file."

"And then what, we all go our separate ways? I don't think so!"

Mia slung the Uzi up and began to spray bullets at about 10 rounds per second through the room, shattering everything, including the sliding glass doors behind her. Glass dropped like rain everywhere. Mia pushed Marisa into Payton and ran through the open door way. Payton shielded Marisa with his body from the flying glass and debris as Mia ran outside into the cover of darkness.

Mia's words echoed in the night air, "Revenge is sweet my friend..."

As Mia retreated down the shoreline, a wave washed Officer Steven's dead body onto the beach.

# Chapter 12

Payton stood upright still holding onto Marisa. He could feel the fear making her body tremble in his arms. Marisa, for a moment, actually felt safe in his arms then she realized whose arms she was in and pushed herself away. The sudden push to Payton's body unleashed what felt like a jolt of electric pain to his side which made his knees want to buckle but he held his ground and grabbed his side. He had a piece of glass lodged in his side just at the edge of his bullet proof vest.

Marisa saw he was bleeding. "You've been shot!"

"No, it's a piece of glass." Payton grabbed Marisa's wrist and guided her hand to his side. "I need you to pull the glass out. Find what direction it went in and pull it out the same way."

Marisa picks up Payton's gun from the floor and points it at him. "Why should I?"

"Because it will save a man's life."

"Yours? Why should I help you?"

"No, the cop's. The one who is about to walk in that door."

"I have your gun."

Payton grabbed Marisa's robe at her waist. "Yeah...but if you don't pull the glass out in the next two seconds, you won't."

"That woman, she said you were partners. Is that true?"

"We served together, we were once a team."

"Sounds like it might have been something more. How could you care about someone as ruthless as her?"

It occurred to Marisa that she had just accused the woman who almost killed them of being a cold blooded killer and the fact that Payton just said they had been a team. Did that mean he was just as cold blooded? If so, why was he protecting her?

Marisa put the gun in her pocket of her robe and moved to Payton's side. All she could see was blood. She picked up the lamp that had fallen onto the floor and adjusted the light. Now she could see the end of the glass reflecting from the lamp. She pinched the end of it and tried to pull it out. The blood made the piece of glass slip out of her fingertips.

"Don't play with it. Just pull it out," Payton quipped.

"I can't get a grip on it. Take off your shirt."

Payton didn't want to compromise his protection by removing his Kevlar but didn't have much of a choice. After removing his vest, he took off his shirt. Marisa grabbed it from him and used it to wipe away the blood around the cut.

"There, that's better."

"Got it?"

"Yes."

Marisa yanked the glass out. At that moment, Officer Morris entered the front door of the living room with his revolver drawn. Payton spun Marisa around and held her from behind. Marisa once again was caught in the middle.

Officer Morris used the wall at the door frame as a shield. "Let her go."

Payton looked to the floor where is Kevlar sat and knew he only had one choice. With his left arm firmly around Marisa's waist, he reached into Marisa's robe pocket with his right and grabbed onto the gun. With the gun still in the pocket of the robe, he slowly raised the gun and pointed it at the officer. In the process he exposed Marisa's long beautiful legs from the top of her thighs down. Marisa did all she could to keep herself from being too exposed but when Payton grabbed her, he pinned her left arm to her side which only left her the ability to barely cover half of herself that was exposed between her thighs as she tried to push the edge of the robe over. Marisa had been naked under the robe and the officer found himself a bit distracted which was Payton's plan all along.

    Payton did his best to keep everyone calm. "I have a gun in my hand. This is what's going to happen. The lady and I are going to leave out the back door here. You are not going to follow us. You poke your head out this door and you're dead. Your Captain, and more than likely your partner, are already dead and someone has to tell their wives. It can be you. We're leaving, don't follow us."

    Payton moved with Marisa in his arms out the door and out of sight. Morris entered the den and had to step over Montano's body to get into position next to the back sliding door. With his revolver clenched in his hands up next to his chest, Morris took one last look at his dead Captain, then took a quick peek out the back door. The darkness was overwhelming and he took a longer look.

With a muffled gunshot, Morris' body fell back next to his Captain's and was just as dead. One shot to the head.

Payton walked Marisa down the beach for about a hundred yards before veering off to a small parking lot. After taking a look around and seeing that the coast was clear, he walked her up to his car. "Get in."

"I just saw you kill a cop. What's to keep you from killing me?"

"I was being paid to kill your husband." Payton lied to keep her from panicking anymore. "Now get in the car before I decide to make Mia's job a little easier."

"Does anyone's life, other than your own, come without a price tag?" Marisa waited for answer but it didn't come. "I didn't think so."

Marisa got in the car. A Jaguar.

Payton drove the two of them up the Pacific Coast Highway.

"My husband is the District Attorney. He is not a killer."

"He may be your husband because you married him but he is definitely one of the bad guys. D.A. and all."

"Why are you doing this? Who are you and what do you and your partner want with a file of my husband's? What is in it that is so important?"

Marisa is sitting crouched in the seat with her knees up to her chest.

"My former partner is Mia Devlin, at least that is what she goes by now, and my name is..."

Before Payton could finish his sentence, Marisa had gripped the seat belt with her left hand and the handle above her with her right and then kicked the gear handle as hard as she could sending it into the park position. The car began to swerve and skid across the road and then over small embankment leaving transmission parts behind in their path. The car came to a full-stop as the weight of the heavy luxury car dug its tires into the sand and eventually parked itself into a sand dune. Marisa undid her seat belt, jumped out of the car, and started to run down the beach. Payton, who was shaken a bit, regained his composure. He saw Marisa as she ran along the shore of the beach and then began to go after her.

After a quick sprint down the beach, Payton overtook Marisa. He grabbed her gently from behind but her twisting motion sent them both toppling into the surf. Payton picked up Marisa, carried her out of the water, and set her down on a dry spot on the beach.

"Listen. Mia was sent here to kill you. From what I can tell, once I did not fulfill my end of the bargain, Delgado must have had her waiting in the wings. I was ordered to help your husband fake his death and put the blame on you."

"I don't understand? Why are they trying to kill you?"

"That must have been the plan all along. Draw me out into the open so Mia could take me out after I did the job."

"I thought she was your partner? Some partner."

Payton removed his hands from around Marisa and noticed blood on his hands.

"You're not the only one who was hit by flying glass."

Payton tried to check Marisa's rib cage by slipping open her robe a little. Marisa pushed his hand away.

"Don't pretend you care."

Payton stood and offered his hand to help Marisa up. At first she refused and tried on her own but the pain is too great.

"Do you want to live to see tomorrow?" Payton asked.

Payton extended his hand once again. This time Marisa accepted and he gracefully lifted to her to her feet. Payton didn't want to fight so he left it up to Marisa and began to walk back to the car on his own. Marisa had too many questions still unanswered and what she saw out of Payton earlier, she knew if she stayed close, she had a better chance of seeing tomorrow. She caught up to Payton holding her side, a bit out of breath and asked, "Who is Jaguar?"

"There is no one named Jaguar. Where did you get that?"

"Our friend, Javier, the Police Captain, asked me if I knew or heard of a man called, Jaguar, which might have pertained to one of my husband's cases."

"That car you just totaled was a Jaguar. My payoff is in that car. That's the only thing I need right now. I don't need you distracting me to the point I let my guard down and then it's lights out."

Marisa started to laugh under her breath. Payton took offense and grabbed her by the collar. But when he looked into her eyes and he saw she wasn't laughing at him but out of fear.

"Why didn't you kill me when you had the chance?"

"You weren't part of the original contract and when it changed at the last minute, I knew there had to be a catch."

"That's why they sent her?"

"Yes."

"I saw you shoot her. Why would you shoot your partner?"

"I know Mia very well. She always wore a vest. You and Montano tell the press your husband is dead and everyone believes the grieving widow. That's why you weren't told about the set up. Realism, real tears, easier to sell it to the press."

"Robert planned this?"

"Yes. Along with Montano. You need to know something, your husband is not dead. He too was wearing a vest."

"How do you know?"

"It was my plan. I was asked to make his death look like you did it before you turned the gun on yourself. The police would see what looked like a murder suicide."

"That's what Javier was trying to tell me when he was killed. He knew something wasn't right."

Payton and Marisa had made their way back to the car. Payton opened the trunk. Inside was a briefcase, a small duffel bag of clothes, and a box of miscellaneous tools. Payton took out a roll of duct tape from the box and tore off a piece.

"We need to clean that cut then put this tape on it for now before it gets any worse."

"Do you have an extra shirt in that bag?"

"Yes." Payton turned his back to get the shirt for Marisa. Marisa turned her back away from Payton, lowered the robe and used the wet robe to clean her wound.

"You kill people for a living and you're telling me I can't trust my own husband because he's a killer. Isn't that some sort of oxymoron?"

"If you say so..."

"So I'm just supposed to trust you, a complete stranger, with my life?"

Payton turned back around with the tape in one hand and a shirt in the other to see Marisa's naked back. Payton used the clean shirt to dry the area around the wound before handing the shirt to Marisa.

"Why should I believe you?"

Payton tore a strip of cloth off the bottom of the t-shirt and set it in the middle of the sticky side of the duct tape. He had Marisa wipe the blood away one more time then placed the make shift field dressing over the three inch cut. Marisa dropped her robe and put on the slightly soiled t-shirt. It was long enough to hang mid-thigh.

"This car was left for me in a parking garage downtown in space 715 along with the directions to your beach house and everything I needed to know about you. This man the police have been after, this Jaguar, is your husband. He's not who you think he is. His real name is Roberto Delgado and he wants you dead."

# Chapter 13

The street lights circling the drive lit up the black limousine as it slowly made its way through the long drive that led up to a brick mansion. Some would call it a small fortress and that was how Robert liked it. He had men stationed about guarding the five acre estate. The limousine stopped at the front entrance. Mia made her way down the steps to meet their guest. Once the car came to a stop, she opened the back passenger door and greeted the guest as he exited the car. "Welcome, Mr. Figari."

Richie Figari stepped from the limousine. When the door closed behind him and the car drove away, it gave him a chill. His first thought was, was this a one way trip? He looked up at the way the amazing brickwork that lines the arch to the entrance of the three story fortress as if he was about to enter the doors of the prison know as Alcatraz. All of a sudden his legs couldn't move. Mia came over and took Richie by the arm and began to walk him toward what felt like his doom. The sound of her voice was too calm. "Mr. Delgado has been expecting you."

≠

Inside the mansion, Sorina was giving her exclusive client a personal massage in the middle of the large den that had been turned into a home fitness center. Robert enjoyed Sorina's company even though she was bought and paid for many times over, she was all woman. Her long beautiful hair flowed off her shoulders and down along the sheer cotton robe she wore that barely covered her at all. She was wearing a devilish smile and a diamond pendant that shined more than her flawlessly tanned skin as it hung around her neck and hung perfectly between her breasts. As she stood at the end of the table working Robert's shoulders, Robert let his hand work her Pilate sculpted thigh just under the edge of her robe. He could feel the heat radiating from her smooth skin as she had just come in from sun bathing nude on the back terrace not thirty minutes ago. His hand followed the back of her thigh all the way up along her curves.

"Sorina, I love what you do for me."

"See, money can buy you happiness," Sorina's voice was as soothing as her hands.

"I take it my money bought you that necklace, too."

"Actually, this is a birthday gift, a date which you never seem to remember."

"From?"

"Does it really matter? I know who my heart belongs to." She hoped that would satisfy him and tried to get him off the subject. "Would you like me to turn on the sauna?"

Before he could answer there was a knock at the door.

"Get that," Robert ordered. Sorina dug an elbow into Robert's naked backside which caused a slight groan from both of them, his from pain, hers from pleasure. Sorina answered the door. As Mia and Richie entered, Sorina made sure Mia got a good look as she adjusted her robe, opening it enough to show Mia a little bit more than just the fact she was wearing the necklace that Mia had given her the night before. Richie got an eyeful as well and hoped his double take wasn't notice by Mr. Delgado.

"Ah, Mr. Figari, I wanted to thank you for coming. You have proven yourself to be very loyal." Robert rose from the massage table and put on a robe that by the looks of it cost more than Richie's entire outfit. In doing so, he turned his back for a moment, long enough for Sorina to slip her robe open along her thigh and in doing so, to give a quick peek to Mia that she was as smooth as silk. Sorina mouthed her appreciation, "Thank you for the necklace."

Richie saw the teasing gesture and walked over to the window to avoid seeing anymore. Robert turned back around and looked to Richie. "Richie, do you know why I invited you here?"

Richie knew his boss didn't need to ask that question, because like most lawyers who ask, he probably already knew the answer. Richie did not answer and did his best to hold it together.

"Richie," Robert's tone was enough.

"I'm sorry, Mr. Delgado..."

Robert put up his hand and Richie froze. Robert didn't like excuses so he changed his mind about the sauna. "Sorina, I'll be ready for that sauna in a minute.

Can you go check go make sure it will be ready in about ten minutes?"

Sorina left the room but didn't close the door all the way. She stood in the hallway to listen.

Robert continued, "Mia, check the hall."

Mia checked the hall, saw Sorina, and gave her a wink. Mia gestured to Robert with a shrug of the shoulders the coast was clear.

With having the room to themselves or so he thought, Robert turned to Richie. "Richie, would like you to do me a favor?"

Richie's voice full of nerves, "A favor, Sir?"

"Yes, a favor. You took the heat for the bust and kept your mouth shut, and for that, I posted your bail. If you do me this favor, you will be rewarded for your efforts as well. We have a very precious cargo to be delivered."

"Sir, the last time I drove for you..."

"Let's leave all that in the past just as long as it doesn't happen again, shall we?" Robert started again after a long pause, "Not only that, how would you like twenty thousand dollars for a single days work? All I'm asking you to do is drive a van from here to Vegas."

Mia chimed in echoing his thoughts, "There you go, Richie, a good score."

Robert added, "Is it my understanding, Richie, that you and Daniela haven't had a proper honeymoon yet?"

"Yes, Sir."

Richie's nerves seemed to stay on edge a bit, the money felt a little too good to be true.

"Well, I want you two to have a memorable honeymoon in Las Vegas on me."

Sorina was still listening in the hallway. She could hear Richie pleading his case to Robert. "Sir, Daniela told me about how grateful she is to be working for you and when I see her tonight, I will tell her what a kind offer you have made but I think she kind of had her mind made up on us taking a cruise for our honeymoon."

"Yes, she seemed to enjoy handling my business when we are on my yacht," Robert's possessive tone caught Richie off guard.

The sorrow on Sorina's face reflected the disappointment in her heart as well. The way she heard Robert speak of Daniela got to her. Robert had told her it was over between them and she was his only pet. She began to fidget with the ring on her finger that Robert had given to her about a two weeks earlier at dinner, as a gesture of his devotion to her.

≠

Marisa was fidgeting with her wedding band as she stood looking out of the window at the ocean that was off in the distance from Payton's hillside home. The moon was full casting its own beacon of light across the water like a beam from a lighthouse that reached up the hillside and painted a light grey veil over the slope leading upward in her direction. It was enough to illuminate the trees and shrubs that decorated the path up to his retreat. She reached into the left bathrobe pocket, removed the pager, and clipped it to the window curtain. The pictures that hung the wall caught her eye and she moved closer to for a better look. It was a Monet.

From behind, Payton watched Marisa intently gaze at the painting, "It's a replica if you were wondering. At least I think it's a replica, that's what the owner tells me."

"So this is not your place?"

"No, it's not. The owner asked me to keep an eye on it until he could find a buyer."

"So, then it is an original."

"Could be. I was just…"

"So you always do as you are asked?"

"I think you know the answer to that one. You're still alive aren't you?"

Marisa didn't want to push any further, for the moment anyway.

"I guess your profession takes you all over the world." Marisa continued down the wall to a set of photographs. A picture of The Eiffel Tower in Paris with the fog rolling in at night, The Louvre Museum in all its glory shot from a nearby hotel window, The Sangrada Famalia in Barcelona Spain with its towers reaching to the deep blue sky.

Marisa knew these were no postcards. "These are yours. You certainly do have an eye for detail. I guess that's what it takes to be a good assassin these days."

"You shouldn't guess so much. My M.O.S. was photography. I just so happened to be an expert with the M-16 which led to the rifle team and then to sniper school. It wasn't long before the shit hit the fan in Central America when we were deployed."

"So how does one go from sniper to assassin overnight?"

"When you're in a fire fight at night that seems to last for a week, you tend to lose count of the hours and the friends you had one minute and then gone the next. The only way out, is to do what you're programed to do. Survive by whatever means necessary."

"And that included turning on your own government?"

"You don't know what happened so don't get all high and mighty on me."

"Then tell me what happened."

Payton holds a first aid kit in one hand a brandy in the other.

"Here, drink this," Payton handed the brandy to Marisa. She took a sip from the snifter made from Waterford crystal. Payton continued, "Maybe another time. We're going to have to remove that tape from your ribs, clean the cut, and add a few stitches to close that wound before you bleed out all over my floor."

Payton encouraged Marisa to take another sip and then another. She began to sip the brandy too quickly and started to choke.

Payton raised her arms above her head. "Take a deep breath and let it out slowly....that's it. Breathe...You don't drink do you?"

Marisa took a shot at killing off the warm smooth liquor but couldn't quite finish it. "Nope..." With one more try, she slammed back the remaining brandy and handed the empty glass to Payton. "One more ought to do it."

"You sure? I wouldn't want you to get too relaxed and not be able to function enough to help me fix you up."

"What do you mean, don't you want me..." she gathers her thoughts as she realizes she has not eaten anything for so long, the brandy is already doing its job just fine. "I mean, what did you give me?"

"It's Courvoisier. Have you ever had it?"

"Ha! No. It sure is smooth…and warm." She looked at Payton in a quizzical way. "So what you are saying is, because I am a woman, I don't have the survival skills like a man? What about that Mia chick?"

Payton walked back over to the wet bar and began to pour Marisa another brandy.

"No, what I am saying is, you shouldn't guess as much. Guessing can get you killed. I'm going to give you a little more you can sip on as we go..."

Marisa began fidgeting with the end of the duct tape that had started to come loose from her side. "Where are we going?"

"Over to the couch so I can get some good light on you to get you stitched up but first we have to get that old bandage off..."

Payton almost dropped the bottle of brandy from the sound of the duct tape being ripped from Marisa's ribs.

# Chapter 14

Robert was leaning back against the front edge of his desk, half sitting on it as he was working a cigar he had just lit. He lets out a good exhale, "I'm afraid, Richie, Daniela is gone. Not to worry, you will be meeting up with her soon."

Richie voice still showing concern, "Is she in Vegas already?"

"She let it slip the other day that the two of you were thinking about wanting to move on, start over. So, I thought as a gesture, I'd give you both a chance to redeem yourselves and get paid handsomely for it. She thought you would be up for such a task so I sent her on ahead. Was she right?"

Richie knew there had to be a catch. "She wouldn't have left without telling me first."

Robert's nonchalant reply was just that, "Then where would be the surprise in that?"

Mia knew she needed to make it at least seem like she was siding with the man who was her boss. "She caught a plane this morning out of Burbank. When

Robert told her about his gift for you two, she knew this could be a nice way to make things up to you."

Robert's tone changed to all business. "I had to send her ahead anyway. The business at hand dictated it. What I am sending up with you can't just be put on a plane so I've arranged a van for you to drive our cargo. You should be joining her soon."

Richie knew something was wrong because Daniela didn't like to fly, "Where is Daniela?"

"She's...gone."

The way Robert said *gone* cut right thru Richie. He jumped out of his chair in Robert's direction. Mia grabbed him by the back of his collar, stopping him before he could get close to Robert.

Richie's voice had a tone of heartache to it. "What did you do to her?"

Robert reply cut even deeper than before, "I guess we're even."

"What are you talking about?

Robert continued, "You did me a favor and I did you one better. She was unfaithful to you."

"No!" More anguish from deep inside Richie.

Robert seem to enjoy torturing Richie. "Yes, she was."

"I'll kill you."

Robert pulled a set of keys out of his pocket and tossed them to Richie. "No, you won't. What you will do is drive the van. If you make a single wrong turn you will be joining our sweet Daniela on a permanent honeymoon."

≠

Marisa and Payton sat on the edge of the couch. Alongside them, on the end table, was a standard military issued corpsman's first aid kit and the make-shift field dressing soaked through with Marisa's blood. Next to that sat a bottle of peroxide, a bowl of warm water and a few small towels, as well as clean bandages with a couple of pieces of medical tape hanging off the edge of the end table.

The true concern in Payton's voice caught Marisa off guard. "Are you ready?"

Marisa found herself staring into Payton's eyes. She played his words over again in her head and they sounded even better than before. She felt them. As drunk as she was getting, the feelings gave her a sobering effect. Payton saw the look in her eyes go from "I don't need you" to "I trust you."

Without a word, Marisa raised the edge of the t-shirt up as far as she could until she flinched from the pain. Payton gently pulled the shirt away from her skin where the blood had dried and held the shirt to her like a band-aide. He slowly lifted the blood stained shirt away from her shapely, well defined figure and then dragged it up over her head and off. Marisa had already crossed her arms to cover her breasts but the shyness she thought she would feel was no longer there.

Payton reached over to a nearby chair and pulled it up close to the couch. His calming voice had gone from giving orders to soothing. "Lie down."

Marisa did her best to lie on her side with her back to Payton as he removed the shade from the lamp on the end table that was next to the couch for better lighting. Payton dipped one of the cloths into the warm water and began wiping away the dried blood as best he could. The water felt warm but the way Payton was carefully cleaning the cut, it felt more like a caress. She knew he was going to protect her from that moment on.

Payton felt Marisa's body relax as he was washing her. He sensed her give in to the fact he was there for her. He too was feeling vulnerable and needed to distract himself to not let his emotions take over. "Glass, as a weapon, is perfect."

It wasn't what she wanted to hear. In a way, she was disappointed. Still holding onto the glass of Brandy, she flipped a wave and with a dash of drunken sarcasm responded, "Yeah, it's wonderful, this brandy sniffer really scares the shit out of me."

"That's a snifter by the way."

Then like a chill that went from his hand on her rib right to her heart she heard the most tender of words come from the man she knew she needed to trust the most. "I don't want you to die."

Marisa couldn't let Payton know how that felt so she jabbed back, "Not until someone pays you to anyway." She felt the regret before she even finished the sentence.

"I didn't take the assignment for the money."

Marisa knew his words were true and it had to do with the other woman, Mia.

"Why does your husband want you dead?" Payton's words were bold and to the point. He listened to Marisa as he began slowly, carefully suturing the wound on her side.

"Some time ago we were at a party and he asked me to go get him a drink. As I was walking away I heard one of his friends say, 'Nice legs, I wouldn't mind having those wrapped around me.' Then my darling husband said, 'Yeah, great legs make for even a greater asset.' That's when I knew I was just his centerfold rather than the center of his life."

Marisa felt the little tug on the suture as Payton tied it off. He then used a clean cloth to wipe away any more blood and to check his work. Marisa rolled back toward Payton. His hand, with the wash cloth, followed the curvature of her body and stopped on her stomach. Marisa's arms folded over her breasts the best she could as well as holding the brandy glass in hand. "So what am I to you? An asset or a loose end?"

Payton slowly slid the wash cloth upward along her stomach, feeling the firm tone of her body under his hand. Payton's voice assuring, "Neither."

Marisa could have used the excuse it was the brandy but she knew what she was doing when she opened her arm for Payton. He slowly continued washing the rest of the sand and blood from off of her. He rinsed the cloth once more, rung it out, then laid the warm cloth back on her smooth skin. He could see her body get the chills as he slid the wash cloth up over her breast. Marisa could feel her heart pounding and her body rise and fall with her breathing as her mind became sharp with anticipation of where his hand was going to caress her next. There was a small bit of dried blood spattered over her heart. Payton could feel his own heart searching for the words he wanted to say but could not as he passed the warm cloth over her other breast. Once he cleaned it off, he was about to withdraw his hand when Marisa put her hand over his and held it over her breast, not letting him move it away.

"What's a human life worth these days?"

"How much value do you put on your own life? I'll give you a clue...it's not a dollar amount. Could you pull the trigger to save your own life? Could you?"

The adrenaline was running through them causing snap decisions to spark off in their minds. Marisa thought about her answer as she took a sip of brandy. Payton took the glass from her and set it on the end table. He waited patiently for Marisa to answer. The way he looked at her at that moment, he knew he was no longer looking at someone who reminded him of Kate—he only saw Marisa.

As she looked at Payton, all she saw was the man, not the assassin. She doesn't even remember saying the words, "I don't know."

The words didn't matter. When Payton heard the tenderness in her voice, he leaned in and kissed her. Time stopped for the both of them. They were no longer the assassin and the target, they were just two people who, for now, needed each other and who no longer wanted to feel alone. Payton could feel Marisa's heart racing as she took her hand away from his, reached up, and put it on the back of his neck. Payton's hand felt like it was floating on the elegance of her skin as he held it there for just a bit longer. Payton sat up and leaned into the sensation of her finger tips as her hand slid away from his neck. Marisa loved the way Payton looked at her with a hunger she too craved, but was it just for tonight or was this just a rogue fantasy with a stranger. Payton saw the reflection of desire in Marisa's eyes that went deep into his soul and he knew from then on, he would do whatever it took to keep her alive, and in his life.

Payton pulled the blanket off the back of the couch and draped it over Marisa. "We need to keep you warm."

It must have been the way he said "we" that had her mind wondering.

Payton continued asking questions as he started cleaning up. "I'm gonna need something from you. Actually, it's in your safe. Can you give me the combination?"

"I don't know the combination."

"Yes, you do. I saw you open it just before the police arrived."

"What is it that you need so bad?"

"I don't know. All I was told was to retrieve a file from the safe."

"Then what?"

Payton knew what he was about to say was no longer the case but he said it anyway, "I was to finish the job and tie up loose ends."

"And I'm the loose end?"

"No, you're not. Not anymore."

Marisa reached back as best she could and took the glass of brandy. "I'm not going to remember any of this in the morning, am I?" Then she finished off the last bit of smooth liqueur from the glass. The alcohol hid her inhibitions. "Why can't I feel anything? Is this how you go through life, not feeling?"

"I'd give my life for you."

"Then my life is in your hands...or not. Make a choice."

Payton leaned in with a tender whisper, "I already have."

Marisa pulled herself up to meet Payton's kiss. The kiss was awkward from the pain she felt but it was a good pain. She never felt more alive. Payton lay her back down on the couch and removed his shirt. He then slid his firm hand down over one of Marisa's thighs. Her skin was so soft compared to the strength of his hands. As he brought his hand back up, he brushed across the velvety texture of her cotton panties. Marisa watched Payton's eyes as they followed his own hand as it caressed and cupped her breast intently. Payton got up out of his chair and shifted over to sit down next to Marisa on the couch as best he could. She bent her legs slightly to give him room on the edge of the couch. Payton slowly slipped her panties down revealing the beauty of her perfectly trimmed love triangle of dark pubic hair. He paused then pulled her panties on down over her long silky legs. She had a few small scars on her calf and around her ankle from her accident. As he gently brushed his fingers over them, Marisa did not feel the shame of the scars but instead felt the tenderness he showed and she could see he was looking at her like no one else had, with compassion.

    Payton slid back on the edge of the couch, leaned in, and kissed her stomach. As they looked into each other's eyes, Payton obliged her request, "Don't stop." Marisa began to run her fingers through his hair. As he kissed, he inhaled deeply, and she could feel his breath being drawn across her skin. She gripped his hair and drove his head lower, guiding his kisses as if each one was a feast of passion. He felt the heat from her on his lips and at the same time her scent overwhelmed his sensibilities.

Payton stood and Marisa watched him as he methodically undid his belt, unbuttoned the fly, and let his faded 501's drop to the floor. Payton sat back down on the couch and took Marisa's hand in his and helped her shift her body onto his lap as she straddled him from her knees.

Payton was ready for her and Marisa was so ready for him. They began to move as one, finding every which way their bodies could conform to one another. He leaned her back and as he did, his tender kisses followed the contour of her neck and then down to her cleavage. Marisa arched her back even more when Payton took one of her nipples in his mouth. A deep moan escaped her lips as she leaned in closer and forced his mouth tighter over her breast. Marisa wanted to taste his lips on hers so badly she gripped the hair on the back of his head and pulled his face back so she could look deep into his eyes. She wanted to see and feel the truth of the moment. He kissed her neck once again and back over to her mouth. Marisa could feel his strong hands grip her ass cheeks and slightly lift her and then lower her back down onto him. Still kissing, that was when he felt her breath hold and then release as her body accepted his.

Just before sunrise Marisa found herself lying on Payton's bed in just a towel. With the effects of the brandy wearing off and the hangover coming on, her head was pounding. Payton exited the bathroom after a quick shower with only a towel wrapped around his waist. He was holding a bottle of aspirin and a glass of water. "Here, you're going to need this."

Payton shook out a couple of aspirin and handed them to her along with a glass of water.

Marisa's words just seem to come out of nowhere, "He made a tape you know."

Payton's reply just as calm, "What tape?"

# Chapter 15

Robert held a stainless steel letter opener in one hand and was cleaning his finger nails on the other as he sat at the edge of his desk. Mia's emotions were being tested between her loyalty to Robert and her thoughts for her lady friend in the hall listening in.

"Mia, I want you to make sure our friend, Mr. Fitch, makes a wrong turn. Lead him to our holding area and make sure our friends on the police force get wind of it. The police want a Jaguar...we'll just have to give them one. I guess it's time to reinvent ourselves once again. Stash the books in the van but before you do, make Vegas the last entry."

"Do you think the books and the drugs will be enough to sell he is this so called, Jaguar?"

"You're right...Sorina's been longing to see the bright lights of Las Vegas. Too bad she will be so close to her dream and only end up on another missing person's list, like so many before her."

All of a sudden, Sorina sauntered into the room pointing a revolver at Robert, Mia had realized she may have just put her friend, Sorina, in the ground with her comments. Mia stepped in front of Sorina, putting herself in between them and put her hand over Sorina's gun that was aimed at Robert, "You don't want to do this."

Sorina pulled the hammer back on the revolver. "I'm going to kill him."

Mia looked over her shoulder at Robert, who had turned his back on them both. "I think she means it."

"She has been known to lie. She's good at it. Her role playing skills have suited us both. She doesn't have it in her." Robert's words seem to always carry an edge to them and this time Sorina was cut deeper than ever before.

Mia felt the hurt in Sorina's body as she held onto her. She could feel her friend shaking with rage from the contempt that came from the void in this man's soul. She saw in Sorina that she had believed Robert when he promised the world but now she knew she felt just like all the others before her. "Her eyes are telling me something different."

"Her eyes have been lying to me for a long time now." Robert did not let up on the spewing of meaningless words to himself but were daggers to his countless women. "It's what she does best, lying. The only reason she's been getting away with it is because she's better at it than the rest."

Sorina tried to quickly step to one side for a clear shot at Robert. As she did, Mia grabbed her arm and forced the gun to fire the shot into the ceiling. In the same motion, the gun was forced from her hand and landed on the floor. Mia stepped Sorina back as Robert picked up the gun and pointed it at Sorina. Before Robert could pull the trigger, Mia, with one punch, knocked Sorina to the ground practically knocking her out.

Robert looked at Sorina and knew she was just another loose end that had to be dealt with. "Put her in the van." Robert grabbed Mia and made it clear he didn't want to see Sorina again. "Take care of her."

Mia helped Sorina off the floor and slowly walked her dazed friend out into the hallway. Sorina knew her fate and asked her friend for one more favor, "Give me your gun."

"He'll kill you."

"I'm already dead."

Mia sat Sorina down on a bench in the hallway and brushed the hair from her face, then, with a gentle wipe, the blood from her lip. The pain was nothing compared to the hurt in her heart. Mia then reached under her jacket and pulled out her gun. "Don't aim for the head, you could miss. Aim for the chest."

"I'm aiming lower."

Sorina gave her friend Mia a kiss goodbye like it was her last then headed back toward the workout room. As she did, Mia wiped away Sorina's blood from her own lip remembering that last kiss. Sorina paused for a moment, looked back at Mia, before entering the room. Sorina turned back to the door and with one last pause she took a moment to pray for the strength to pull the trigger. Mia watched Sorina as she took one more deep breath before she opened the door. Mia's feelings for her friend Sorina raced through her mind and as she got closer to the room she could hear Sorina's cold but determined anger in her voice cut through the air, "Turn around and look at me, you bastard! Look at me!

Before Mia could reach the doorway, one gunshot silenced the house as it echoed through the halls. Mia waited then felt the horror when she saw Sorina back out of the room with the stainless steel letter opening sticking out of her chest. Sorina was bleeding out as she fell back into Mia's arms. In the silence, every sound seemed to be enhanced. The sound of Mia's gun falling on the wooden floor of the hallway amplified as it tumbled just out of reach. Even Sorina's staggered shallow breaths from having been stabbed in the chest seemed to reverberate in the small space.

Sorina looked into Mia's eyes, "It's never painless...is it?" With her dying words she kissed Mia one last time. Mia gently lay Sorina's body on the ground. Even in death Mia could see the beauty that was Sorina. With the blood from their last kiss still on her lips, Mia took her finger and rubbed it fully across her lips, and then she kissed Sorina on the forehead leaving a pattern of her lips in blood.

Robert was running his finger through the hole in his robe below his crotch area where Sorina had missed her target. She had managed to miss any part of Robert as her shot had passed right between his legs. She hadn't aimed high enough. Soon Robert's curiosity got the best of him of why wasn't Mia coming back. There was just too much silence that seemed to draw his attention out into the hallway. He reached back into the cigar box for his gun.

Robert found himself alone in the empty hallway except for Sorina's lifeless body lying on the floor. Robert looked down the hall at the door leading out the back of house and could only feel the loss of control. "Mia! You're dead, you know that, you're dead!"

Mia stepped from behind the door of the workout room with her gun pointed at Robert. "If you so much as twitch, I'll kill you."

Robert hesitated then let his fingers relax, allowing his gun to drop to the floor. The gun landed near Sorina's body in a small pool of her blood. Mia stepped forward and pushed Robert away from Sorina's body. Mia dropped to one knee next to Sorina and removed the necklace from around Sorina's neck, a gift Mia had given to her part-time lover.

Two armed body guards rushed into the hallway from the other doors, guns drawn, and immediately flanked Robert on each side like two book ends. Robert didn't seem to miss a beat when it came to twisting a verbal dagger, "Don't ever fall in love."

Mia wasn't stressed out about the guns that were pointed at her as long as she had her steady hand aimed at Robert's head. "After I'm finished with Payton, I will find you and you will learn what it means..."

Robert interrupts Mia, "What, the meaning of love?"

Mia walked right up to Robert, not paying any attention to the book ends and put the end of her gun right over Robert's cold heart. "What it means to die."

Mia backed away and worked herself down the hall, Robert's callous demeanor caused her to pause. Robert, without a care, motioned to the body guards to remove Sorina's body. "Put the body in the van, she's served her purpose."

Upon hearing Robert's heartless orders, Mia stopped and raised her gun back on Robert. But this time, her emotions did come to the surface as the gun in her hand slightly shook but she was able to keep her anger in check.

Robert's tongue flicked like a serpent's. "Mia, it's not like you to get all worked up over nothing."

"As much as you use people, you should know everyone has something to offer...and she was something."

"She had nothing when I found her. Everything about her, my money created. I made her. She was mine to do with as I pleased. What right do you think you have to take something of mine?"

Mia turned and walked away and as her pace quickened she came to a set of large double wooden doors. Just as she slammed open the doors with such power to cause a loud bang that combined with the bright light from outside consumed the hallway, Robert yelled one last dig, "She was nothing!"

≠

As the morning light passed through the bedroom window, it gave the room a glow of peaceful serenity. Suddenly Marisa sat up in bed and realized she was not in her own bed, causing an instant head rush from her hangover. She had to lay her head back down on the pillow. The clock on the night stand read 10 A.M. Next to the clock was a couple more aspirin and a glass of water. Marisa sat up, took the aspirin, and noticed she was wearing a large souvenir t-shirt from Paris.

Marisa was reminded of the previous night by her blood stained robe that sat on a wooden chair across the room beyond the end of the bed. Sticking out of one of the robe's pockets was her underwear. Marisa stood straight up on the bed and quickly raised the t-shirt to expose the fact she was wearing a pair of Payton's boxer shorts. She smiled.

Marisa passed her finger tips over her bruised ribs and felt the stitches that Payton had so attentively sutured. She carefully took a seat on the end of the king sized bed and felt not only the warmth from the sun on her back but the memory of the night before. She couldn't believe she had made love with Payton but her body had told her otherwise, it was true. She lay back on the bed and ran her hands over her body, triggering her body's memory of Payton's firm hands caressing her. His hands were so strong but they seemed to glide over her skin like a melted butter. Although her heart rate was rising, she could sense the silence in the house. The sense of being alone all of sudden became real and her life was no longer what she thought it was. She got up and made her way into the living room. Once again Marisa couldn't help but study Payton's photographs that hung on the walls of the spacious living space. She fanned her finger tips across a small set of pictures on the coffee table, spreading them out evenly. The pictures were of her on the beach, in her home, and at the market. Across the room, Marisa saw a full length wooden framed mirror on casters. She angled it front of the window to allow more light to shine into the room. While in front of the mirror, she playfully modeled herself in the boxer shorts. Marisa was interrupted by the pager going off. BEEP. BEEP. BEEP. Marisa unclipped it from the curtain and checked the number.

It read: *729866*.

Marisa went to the phone that hung on the wall next to the kitchen, removed it from the cradle and looked at the numbers that coincided with the numbers on the bottoms on the receiver. She looks at the six numbers and the three letter options that went with each number and wrote down the corresponding letters for each. PRS, ABC, and so on. Marisa began to circle one letter in each group to spell, Payton. The pager sounded again and displayed the same number.

# Chapter 16

Payton hung up one of the few working pay phones in the area and walked away a bit at odds with himself. Usually when he sent Robert a page to make contact it was to say, "We need to meet" or "The job was finished." This time was to let him know he was done and if he came after him, it wasn't going to end well. He walked over to the local newsstand on the way back to his car to pick up the current morning edition of the *L.A. Times* newspaper and tucked it under his arm. Payton climbed into his black Porsche and tossed the paper on the passenger seat in exchange for the file that laid there. He flipped open the file and programmed the address at the top of the page of the lease into his GPS then started the engine and entered into traffic. He immediately passed a red Trans Am that was parked a few spaces ahead. As Payton's car drove passed, Mia sat up in the front seat, started her car, and began to follow Payton a few car lengths behind.

Payton pulled his car up to the curb across from a small warehouse with a gas station out front. It was definitely a privately owned station and from the looks of it, the business made most of its profits from detailing cars which meant it could also be a front for a chop-shop. There were a few fender benders out front but the high-end work was being done inside the open bay doors.

Payton parked across the street to watch the activities at the station. He saw a man answer the phone inside the shop who then gestured to one of the mechanics down in the pit who then tossed up a clear plastic bag taped up. He sent it up to another attendant who immediately stopped his work, turned, and used the tire re-placement machine to slip the kilo package inside the tire and re-sealed the tire, added air and then pull a decoy tire off the wall that was located on the inner wall of the cinder block garage bay. The mechanic down in the pit repeated the procedure and got two tires ready for the exchange before he headed to a tow truck that was standing by out front. Payton had a good idea what was in the package and decided to follow the tow truck. Just as he started his car to follow, Mia pulled her Trans Am up next to Payton's car, and blocked him in.

Mia lowered her passenger window and drew a bead on Payton with her silenced .22. "I'll tell you what...finish the contract on Marisa and we'll call it even."

Payton didn't have to think about it. "You know that's not going to happen."

A short blast of a siren from a police car that had pulled up behind Mia's car changed her immediate plans. "We both know she has to die, Payton."

The officer couldn't see the gun drawn on Payton as she was using the headrest of the passenger's seat to shield it from view. Mia lowered the gun, laid it in the seat next to her, and drove on ahead. The police car then pulled forward and slowly passed Payton to observe Payton's reaction. Payton didn't pay any attention to the police officer as he passed by but instead kept his eye on Mia as she turned left about two blocks ahead. Payton observed the police car on her tail as it made the same turn. Payton then pulled out into traffic and decided to drive straight on ahead rather than to follow. Payton drove his car through a giant pothole full of water that splashed its muck onto the tires of a nearby tow truck hauling a large van that had a nice set of chromed, baby moon hubcaps.

≠

Marisa wiped the mist from the shower that had fogged the bathroom mirror and revealed her wearing two towels, one around her body and the other on her head. She dropped the body towel and saw the reflection of the stitches Payton had sutured on her side. She ran her fingertip across the four tightly crisscrossed X's and thought to herself that she wouldn't even mind if it left a scar because she knew she would always want to remember that night and how it changed her life forever. She got dressed in a set of her own clothes, removed the towel from her head, shook out her hair, and used her fingers to brush out her hair allowing her finger tips to skim along her neck as another reminder of the way Payton had touched her the night before, bringing a smile to her face. Marisa turned off the light and headed for the living room. As Marisa entered the living space, Payton handed her the re-heated cup of coffee he had brought her back from Starbucks and tossed the newspaper he had been reading onto the coffee table.

"Thanks for the coffee." She took a sip of the overpriced brew, "How did you know I like sugar in my coffee?"

"I didn't. This one's black, just in case you didn't."

"Thank you again and for also bringing back a few of my things. Did you enjoy going through my drawers?" Payton hesitated long enough not to answer before Marisa had another question and from look on his face, he wasn't about to anyway. "Speaking of which...last night, did I undress myself or did you?

That brought a smile to Payton's face. "You don't remember?

"No..."

Payton didn't know if she was having fun or not but he played along and changed the subject once again as he pointed to his side. "How are your stitches holding up?"

Before Marisa could answer, something on the TV caught Payton's attention and he grabbed the remote, turning up the volume. The news was on and it confirmed the newspaper front page. Payton open opened up the newspaper and flipped it around so Marisa could see the bold type. "Check this morning's headlines."

The headline read:

L.A. POLICE CAPTAIN MURDERED!
D.A. AND WIFE MISSING

Marisa still didn't understand why her husband wanted her and Capt. Montano, dead. "Why would he have his best friend killed?"

"You amaze me. Your husband wants you dead and you are more concerned about Montano. Montano was playing a Bishop to a King. This King only cares about one thing, staying King, and he cares even less about his Queen."

Marisa saw something in Payton, his passion for her, and how he would not have let anything happen to her if she was his. It even caught Payton by surprise, how he spoke about her, so protective. Payton shut off the television. The silence was deafening.

Marisa felt Payton's declaration, let him off the hook and changed the subject. "What did you find in the safe? Did you find the file?"

"The file was gone. Robert must have given the combination to Mia. The safe did have something interesting though. A deed to a gas station."

"My husband doesn't own a gas station."

"You're right. He doesn't...but you do. You were working on a story that was about to lead you, back to you."

"Me?"

"If you had stayed on track, you were about to link your husband to a drug cartel that is based out of..."

"El Salvador. Yes, my lead was about to expose a new player in this ever changing landscape of the cocaine market here in southern California. Mainly their distribution tactics. Are you telling me the gas station, which is in my name, is a part of it?"

"Yes, your gas station. They're using the tow trucks to do business right out in the open. Your husband has it registered in your name."

Payton pulled the folded manila envelope out of his back pocket and showed Marisa the deed.

"What about the recording I saw of Robert being shot by you?"

"Didn't have time to find it. The police arrived and..."

"Don't tell me. First you hid in the attic until they were gone, then you grabbed a few things for me before you left, and on the way back you stopped to get a paper and called your boss."

"You left out the part about running into Mia and her wanting you dead."

"And you said?"

"Nothing."

"Nothing?" Marisa was now defending the connection she thought her and Payton now had.

Now it was Payton's turn to let Marisa off the hook, "Our conversation was interrupted."

"Try calling the pager again"

"I can't. The call could be traced back to here. That is why we use the pager. Less likely to be traced."

Marisa heads over to the window to retrieve the beeper. She caught Payton's reflection in the full length mirror when she said, "Don't tell me. You don't plug in a phone number, you plug in the numbers that spell, Payton, letting my husband know you needed to meet."

"Yes. How did you know?"

Marisa turned back toward Payton just as the full length mirror exploded from a rifle shot from across the street that passed through the six inch gap in the curtains that hung in the bay window. Payton knew exactly what had happened and what was about to happen again. Just as he reached over and pulled Marisa to the ground, he had been expecting a second shot, but there was no shot.

"Stay down!"

Payton picked up a piece of broken mirror and kicked what was left of the mirror back out of the line of sight of the window and used the small piece of mirror to look out the window but didn't see anyone. "Mia is slipping. She shot your reflection instead of you. Now that she thinks you're dead and she'll be coming after me, that's good."

"If I'm dead...why am I shaking?"

"Because you're still alive."

Payton helped Marisa to stand up and pulled her over in front of the fireplace to keep her out of sight. He had her in his arms when he showed her his gun. "Do you trust me?"

Marisa nodded.

"There's no need to be afraid if you can pull the trigger."

Marisa looked at Payton, giving him a look that came straight from her heart. She trusted him with her life. Payton handed Marisa his Beretta.

"Where are you going?"

"To take a look around. I'm sure she's gone but I still want to be sure."

Payton kissed Marisa quickly but it was enough to distract her and assure her he would come back. When Marisa heard the front door close leaving her all alone that is when it hit her, that feeling of not just being alone but of missing someone. She had not felt that way in a long time. It had only been a couple of days, one day she thought she had it all only to find out she had nothing and the next, she was on the run with a man she just met and never felt more alive. She heard the front door open and realized her adrenaline had amped up her senses and she was able to feel her breathing start up again when she saw Payton heading her way.

"Are you okay?" His attention for her was never more heart felt. "Come with me, I want to show you something."

Payton began to lead Marisa away but she stopped him for a moment, "Payton."

"Yes."

"About last night. I do remember. Everything."

"Well, I hope it is not our last and to ensure that it wasn't, there is something I need you to do."

# Chapter 17

Payton had converted one wing of the wine cellar into a firing range. He opened a cabinet exposing a variety of hand guns, knives, a rifle, an Uzi, and assorted weaponry. "What's your vintage? How about this one?" Payton pulled a 9mm Beretta and handed it to Marisa. "It should be to your liking. It's just like the one you pulled on me in your husband's den."

"I see you have a few of them. It must be your favorite weapon."

"I guess it is but nothing like making a shot from over a mile away with a M107 50 caliber sniper's rifle."

"And I thought you said glass was your favorite weapon."

"It is, but for a different reason."

"Why glass?"

Payton pulled a wine bottle from a rack to use as an example. "The human body has very little resistance to it, it's quick, it's usually readily available, and it's disposable."

"What do you do at night? Lie awake and think of what a poor childhood you must have had and how to get even?"

Payton takes a moment. "You have a lot of sleepless nights when falling asleep may get you killed. You wonder what kind of country trains you, sends you to a place not on any map, leaves you for dead, and then says you were never there."

"You said us. How many?"

"There were two teams of two sent in. Each team made up of a shooter and a spotter. We assumed the other team didn't make it because Delgado is still alive. That left Kate and me. She was my spotter."

"So that's where your pact was made."

"The next thing you know you're fighting to stay alive and fighting your way out the only way you know how."

"As assassins?"

"At first it was just me. Delgado had Mia and was using her as leverage to take out his competition. I just did what I had to do to keep Kate alive."

"Kate? You mean, Mia?"

"Yes, Kate goes by Mia now. It's a long story."

"Tell me."

"No, not now anyway."

"She was more than your spotter, you cared for her. I can hear it in your voice, the way you say her name. Your tone changed when you referred to her as Mia."

"How close were you?"

"I know her... Let's just say, I know her well enough to know she always wears a vest and that's why I'm still alive."

"Because she still has feelings for you?"

Payton didn't have an answer for Marisa.

Marisa saw another part of Payton she was becoming more and more interested in, his feelings. "What about family? Are your parents still alive?"

"Forgotten."

"You're afraid by contacting them you would lead Mia to them."

"Something like that. Their lives depend on me not knowing."

"So I guess this means you don't have anyone, do you?"

Marisa gave Payton a smile that said, "Except me."

Payton handed Marisa a pair of ear muffs and a clip for her gun, "You're going to need these." Payton hung a pair of ear muffs around her neck. He then positioned himself and Marisa at the end of the makeshift firing range. Payton put his hands over Marisa's and went through a few instructions. "This is the safety. It's in the 'on' position. This is the clip release." Payton thumbed the release button and the clip fell out.

"I do know that much."

"Do you know how to pull a trigger and kill a man?"

Marisa looked at Payton and her eyes give her answer away. "No."

Payton shoved the clip back into place and then thumbed the release back down. "Now you're ready to fire." Payton once again turned Marisa's body facing down the hall and helped her to put on ear protection and then his own. "Can you hear me?"

Marisa nodded. Payton wrapped his arms around her, took hold of her hands, helped to unload and load the clip into the gun, and then helped her to take aim down the forty foot range.

"I want your arms straight out and locked. I want you to make your shoulders rigid and lock your hips. Now look over the top of the gun through the sites, then at your target. You can do this. I have the target set at 20 yards. The average person can be effective at 25 so you will be fine at this range. People have a tendency to aim too high and anticipate the kick so lower your aim just a bit."

Marisa closed one eye and took aim over the gun sites and in doing so, cocked her head slightly as she lowered her hands a bit.

"You'll be fine, I've got you. On my mark, I want you to slowly pull the trigger. When it goes off, it should be a surprise. Go ahead, fire."

Marisa fired the gun. She missed the target that was in the shape of a silhouette of the upper half of a man completely but hit the end of the paper.

"It's best to keep both eyes open."

Marisa open both eyes and centered herself.

"That's better. You can't hit what you don't see."

Payton hit the safety on the gun then went to a nearby cabinet, reached in, took out a silencer, and attached it to the gun.

"Let's try it again."

Marisa got ready, released the safety, and fired once more to only the supression of the silencer. She caught the edge of the silhouette near the shoulder.

"This time pull the trigger in between breaths. Just after the exhale and before the inhale."

Marisa takes a deep breath then exhales.

"Hold it. Now..."

Marisa didn't remember pulling the trigger but the sound of the "piff" from the silencer and the jump in her hand from the Beretta happened so fast, all she saw was a slight ripple in the paper of the target. "I don't see where I hit the paper."

"That's because you're not in the white. You hit the black of the silhouette."

"Really?"

Payton began to slowly back away from Marisa as she fired another round. Marisa was comforted with the feel of Payton's body behind her so before he could get too far away, she reached back with her left hand and grabbed Payton by the hip and pulled him closer, urging him the stay up close behind her.

Marisa never felt so safe than in his arms. She squeezed off another round then another. Payton could smell Marisa's perfume start to rise from her as her body temperature was also on the rise. Payton kissed her shoulder. She fired another round. Payton parted his lips and kissed her firmer, tasting her skin. She fired another round. Payton slipped his hand around her waist and he slowly slid it up across her torso to her breast. He could feel her breathing getting stronger.

"You shouldn't let anything distract you, Marisa."

Marisa hit the safety and turned to Payton with tears in hers eyes. "I can't do it."

"Listen to me. If anyone ever points a gun at you, they intend to use it. When you pointed the gun at me last night, you hesitated. The next time you do that, you're dead."

The finality in Payton's words hit a cord in Marisa. "I don't think I'll ever be able to pull the trigger. A target is one thing but..."

"I don't want you to die."

To Marisa, Payton's plea was never more heartfelt.

"If Delgado has his way, he's not going to stop until you are dead, so you better get on board with the idea it's you or them."

Payton pulled a light weight bullet proof vest from another drawer and slipped it on. He then put a new, full clip in the gun.

"Don't think about it. Just do it."

Payton moved into the firing tunnel. He was about fifteen feet away.

"Shoot me. Aim for my lower chest area. Those small practice loads won't penetrate, even this close."

The lighting in the tunnel turned Payton into a silhouette just like the target. Marisa put the gun down on the counter. Payton moved in on Marisa and grabbed her by the collar.

"Pick it up."

"Go to hell."

Payton lowered his head, "I got news for you," then looked up and gazed into Marisa's eyes and offered her the truth as he knew it, "it turns out, heaven and hell are both on earth, you just have to decide which on you want to live in."

"I hate you. I hate the way you make me feel."

"Good. Now please, pick up the gun."

Marisa slowly picked up the gun.

"Aim for the chest. Forget the head, if you only get one shot, you'd better slow them down."

Payton moved back to his position in the tunnel. Marisa took aim.

"Why are you making me do this?"

"Because Mia is not going to stop until either she kills you or kills me first and then comes after you. I, for one, would prefer that neither of those things happen today."

"What if Mia is wearing her vest? What happens if I shoot her and she gets up?"

"Then I guess you can take the head shot."

Marisa took aim at Payton's chest. "What if I miss the vest and hit you?"

"Keep both eyes open, breath normally, and slowly squeeze."

"How is this normal?"

"If I didn't believe in you, I wouldn't be standing here."

For Marisa that somehow made sense and in that moment, she didn't think and she pulled the trigger. The silencer rang out its "piff" and sent Payton flying backwards into the darkness of the floor.

Marisa stood there in shock. She had just shot a man. Her words were caught in her throat but she was able to force them out, "Tell me you're still alive?"

There was what seemed like the longest pause in between Marisa's heart beats when she heard Payton answer from the floor, "I lied...that hurt."

"Are you alright?"

Payton stood up, removed the vest, leaned in and gave Marisa a kiss. "How about you wear the vest next time?"

"Is it that easy for you? What if I killed you?"

Payton grabbed the front of her collar once more and she felt the anger in his focused rage, "Yes...it's that easy, and you would have been doing me a favor."

Marisa had the gun pointed at Payton's mid-section. The gun was close but not touching. Payton relaxed his grip. "Control your heart and your mind will follow. If you lose it, you're dead."

Marisa lowered the gun. "Is it always life or death with you? Aren't you afraid of living wondering when the extremes will eventually catch up with you?"

Payton pondered the question for a second. "And if they do, I will welcome them."

"And in the mean time?"

Payton saw the fear he had put into Marisa's eyes and as much as he wanted to take it away, he felt it would keep her alive. But Payton's heart was telling him something else and he kissed her and caressed her so hard, he could feel her legs buckle beneath her. Marisa allowed her body drop into the safety of Payton's arms. She felt the weight of the world come off of her and she let her body give in to her desires and it felt so right.

Marisa's thoughts escaped her, "Tell me this is for real."

"I'm not going anywhere."

When Marisa heard Payton's reply, she realized she had been living a lie for so long and for the first time understood she was just a pawn in someone else's game and the only safe harbor was in Payton's arms.

Payton sensed the anxiety from her open prayer, "Promise me something."

Payton could feel Marisa's heartbeat pounding as fast and in rhythm with his as she finished her thought, "Promise me, tomorrow."

Payton knew one thing, he wanted it with her as well and even though he knew there were no guarantees, he had to let her know how he felt, "I promise."

The skirt Marisa was wearing was at mid-thigh and easily rode up as she raised her leg and wrapped around Payton. Payton reached down, caressed her thigh and as he did, he pushed the skirt up even higher. He slid his hand up under her skirt and felt her panties as an enticing barrier. He palmed his hand over them and gripped her firmly from behind. Their kisses became harmonious and tender, giving and taking, each one brought them closer to a sense of urgency as their hearts longed for one another. She reached down between them and undid Payton's belt and flipped the buckle back. She found the top button of his jeans and worked each button down, one after another. She felt his breath waver over her mouth as her hand rubbed over his briefs and found him so hot and firm for her.

Marisa shoved her hand deep into his briefs, as far as she could reach as she felt Payton tug at her panties.

Just as she wrapped her fingers around him, Payton's grip tore away one side of her panties. She felt the desperation they both craved and she guided him between her thighs. Payton pulled down the rest of her shredded panties and Marisa could feel them slide down her leg as he lifted her off the ground. As she wrapped her legs around Payton's waist, she flicked her panties from off her ankle onto the floor. Marisa looked into Payton's eyes and with each thrust she was becoming his. She wanted nothing more than to have him desire only her. She felt Payton's body start to swell with passion as he cradled her in his arms. With such grace he guided her up and down, deeper with each breath, allowing her body to give into the wave she felt coming on so strongly.

They felt the immense satisfaction as it grew and their bodies clung to one another. Payton's deep groan reverberated through Marisa as he exploded into her causing Marisa to let out a moan of her own, accepting the wave that was unleashed from deep within as it began to roll upward through her body. Marisa began to shake and quiver in Payton's arms. He held her tightly against him and rode the surge of euphoria with her. When they each caught their breath, they kissed once more, sealing their promise to one another once more.

Payton lowered Marisa to the floor and gently brushed her damp hair that was clinging to the side of her face and away from her eyes, "I hope you believe me now when I say…"

Marisa put a finger to Payton's lips. "I believe you."

Payton reached over and picked up the Beretta and handed it to Marisa, "Stay focused." He picked up her torn panties off the floor and put them in his pocket then kissed her once more and walked away.

Marisa turned and faced the silhouette, released the safety, and took aim. Marisa fired a round then feeling the power of the moment, her eyes begin to fill with tears from all the mixed emotions from the last twenty four hours. Payton stopped in the doorway and took a look back at Marisa and took a deep breath that felt like joy on the way in and sadness on the way out.

Marisa did her best to hit the silhouette but a few went astray. Payton saw the effort and the fear in her stance as she did her best to keep firing on target, but was it going to be enough?

# Chapter 18

Payton entered the living room holding Marisa's blood stained robe from the previous night and assessed the room from the perspective he anticipated Mia would have used. His eyes scanned the room looking for clues that needed to be left to sell the idea Mia had done her job and taken out her target. He pushed the mirror back away from the window then placed Marisa's robe on the floor in its place. Payton then picked up a shard of glass and sliced the edge of his left palm just enough to draw some blood. He squeezed his hand and dripped out a few drops of blood onto the floor here and there to help sell the idea Marisa was hit.

Marisa walked into the room and saw Payton trying to paint the floor with a few drops of his blood. "What are you doing?"

"If we want Mia to believe you're dead, we're going to need a blood trail."

"If that's the case, wouldn't there be more blood?"

"Not if the kill shot was to your heart. Your heart would have stopped pumping the blood out. And if I was nearby and got to you quickly enough to try to save you, my actions would be to cover your chest with something preventing even less of a blood flow so, no, not really."

Payton then grabbed a piece of the belt off of Marisa's robe and wrapped around his cut. "Ready?"

"Ready for what?"

"We can't stay here. Mia will soon be here to confirm her kill."

"Where are we going?"

"It doesn't matter. We just need to leave now. Come here. I need you to stand by the blood."

As she made her way toward Payton, Marisa did her best to avoid stepping in any of the blood. "Now what?"

"Lean back into me."

As she does, Payton dragged Marisa's heals through the blood and created a smeared blood trail toward the front door. On the way out, Payton kicks over a few things as if leaving in haste and just before the door, Payton picked Marisa up and carried her out.

The night air surrounding the Beach House Hotel was cool. The fog horn sounded as the heavy mist seemed to roll in like a magic carpet as it drew in off the ocean and brought a nice glow to the exterior lighting of the entrance to the hotel. The way Payton had driven his way up to the quiet coastal getaway had a style to it. He had been there before and knew what to expect, plus he liked the ability to make a quick exit along the beach.

Pulling up front, the valet opened the door for Marisa when the car stopped. As she stepped out, she took in a deep breath of that ocean air she loved so much, she could hear the cry of the seagulls as they glided above in the muted orange hues of the sunset as it was fading away. The valet had made his way to the driver's door. Payton exited the car and gave the younger man a simple smile.

The valet knew that smile. "I know, scratch it, and I'm dead."

Inside the lobby of the seasoned hotel, Marisa took a quick look around to make herself familiar with her surroundings before she joined Payton at the front desk. The lobby was decorated with a bit of the old as well as looking new. A few antique pieces of furniture along with some glass fishing floats of different colors and sizes dressed up the lobby. The old roll top desk had what seemed to be an old ledger from a ship that had a drawing resembling buried treasure.

The desk clerk went over the registration card Payton filled out.

"Mr. and Mrs. Scanlan, welcome. I see you are staying one night, okay. Can I please see one form of picture ID and I'll need a major credit card for any additional incidental charges, please?"

Payton fanned out five one hundred dollar bills onto the counter, and then smiled at Marisa. "I got it, honey." Payton turned back to the desk clerk. "That should cover it, yes?"

Before the desk clerk could answer, the owner stepped in, "Hello, Mr. Scanlan, nice to see you again. It's been a while."

"Yes, nice to see you too, Laurie."

Laurie took the cash and made Payton a receipt. "Are you staying long?"

"Just one night. Is the kitchen still open?"

"Yes. I will let them know you are here. We have two rooms available, one in the back or one looking over the ocean. It was a cancelation so I can give you a good deal on that one."

"Yes, that'll work just fine."

"I'll have someone show you to your room."

"Thank you, Laurie. It was nice to see you again."

As Payton and Marisa crossed the lobby, Marisa took a glance back and saw Laurie still looking at Payton. "Come here often? She seems to have her eye on you."

"When I need to be alone, I come here, walk the beach, have a drink and try to forget."

"Forget what?"

"My life."


The bellman opened the door for Marisa and Payton then followed them into their spacious room. There was a dividing wall that separated the living space from the bedroom but it only took a glance to see there was only one queen bed. The décor was what you would have expected, standard sunset colors and matching window curtains.

Payton was all about keeping a low profile and whispered to Marisa, "Don't do anything to draw attention."

The bellman began to give his best spiel to maximize his tip, "Welcome to..."

Payton didn't need to hear it, cutting off the bellman stating, "That will be fine, thank you," and handed the bellman a ten dollar bill. He wanted to send him on his way but Marisa had other ideas. All this fake dying had her starving and was taking a look at a room service menu. "What's the most expensive thing on the menu?"

Payton gave Marisa a look of, "Whatever happened to low profile?"

Marisa smiled and tossed the menu onto the desk.

$$\neq$$

Mia dropped a series of black and white photographs of Marisa onto the coffee table. She held onto one of an eight by ten head shot of Marisa and walked over to the window where her round had pierced the glass. Marisa's blood stained robe was lying on the floor. Mia took a look around where Marisa had been standing. She followed the blood trail and saw where Payton must have tried to save Marisa and the drag marks where he whisked her across the floor away from the line of sight of the window. She took one more look at her picture then tore the picture in half and let it drop onto Marisa's robe. The two halves fell very close to each other. The top half of Marisa's face just above the bottom half with its white back facing side up.

$$\neq$$

Marisa took a deep breath as she wiped her mouth with her white linen napkin as the two of them had just finished their room service dinner of a Sourdough Bread Bowl filled with Clam Chowder, a Crab Louie Salad, and Grilled Salmon on a bed of Pesto Sauce. The plates were empty and not much was left of the bread bowl let alone the bottle of wine. Marisa took the last of her wine over to the window to sip and wait for Payton's answer.

"I think most people instead of running for the truth would rather walk in a lie. It's just easier."

"If you're such an expert on lying, why are lies so easy to believe and the truth so hard to accept?"

"Because what most people want to hear isn't always the truth."

"Are you even capable of telling the truth?"

"You wouldn't know if I was."

"Try me."

Payton took a moment to ponder himself then, "On my thirteenth birthday, my father took me hunting, and of course he brought along our dog, Bullet. Bullet got a bit ahead of us on the trail as my father was telling me to watch the top of the trees for the wind direction. All of a sudden he kicks a rattle snake resting under some brush on the edge of the trail we were on."

"Is that how your father died?" Payton gave her a look. "Sorry, what happened next?"

"What happened was so fast and in slow motion at the same time. I remember my father pushing me away, the sound of the snake rattling its tail, then striking my father in the leg. The next thing I know Bullet has the snake in his mouth trying to shake the fucking life out of it."

"Bullet killed the snake?!"

"Yeah, he did...but not before getting bit also. Next thing I know I have my father's rifle in my hands and he's telling me not to let Bullet suffer any more than he has to. The rest is a blur except for me having to drive down off the mountain. I can't even remember how I found the Hospital.

"Did you make it in time to save your father?"

"Yeah, but cancer got him about three years later."

"Was that the last time you got to spend any quality time with him?"

"We made it back one more time after that. We came across the same trail where it all happened. I'll never forget my father spending a round out of his rifle and leaving it lay there in memory of Bullet."

"I saw you do the same thing before you went to go after Mia. I also found the round you left on my balcony. You were there to kill me?"

"Is that so hard to believe?"

"So what kept you from finishing the job?"

"Kate."

Payton went to the bed, unzipped one of his duffle bags then began to remove a change of clothes. Payton knew he had to tell Marisa everything. "Kate…Kate and I were a team. I was the shooter and she was my spotter. I knew we had feelings for each other but we had to stay focused while we were deployed. I told her I had someone back home but I don't think she believed me, but she seem to understand, and we stayed the course. Then once we were captured, Delgado got to her in ways you don't want to know about and if I can help it, you will never have to experience." Payton then removed a shoulder holster already strapped with a pistol and tossed it on the bed.

Marisa had to ask, "Why do you call her Mia now?

"In order to survive, she became Mia."

"Do you still love her?"

Payton looked at Marisa and she saw hurt in his eyes and understood the woman he once loved was no longer. "When you look at me now, what do you see? Are you looking at me through a scope or the lens of your camera?"

"It not about you. Most people just live to get by and buy everything they see to make themselves feel good. Take off the blinders and see what is really happening here. Everything has a price and most just choose not to admit it."

"At least what I see doesn't have a blood money attached to it. I've been working for everything I have."

"Oh really. You're a photojournalist who just happens to be lucky enough to get a prime spot on a leading newspaper your first job right out of college."

Marisa was shocked Payton knew so much about her. "I'm good at what I do."

"You're a great photographer but as a journalist, you got a little help from your husband who's in bed with a few of the wrong people who are in the right places, and guess what? It almost got you killed." Marisa still seemed to be in the dark. "The current story you are researching now, where do you think it's going to lead? You just happened to find a lead or was it given to you?"

"My husband was on a case and gave me the story after one of his cases led to a drug trafficking ring."

"Yes. He gave you a lead that would get you fucking killed."

"I hate that word."

"I don't mean to offend your sensibilities but sometimes it just fits."

Marisa looked at Payton with a new perspective and Payton could see the wheels turning in her mind. He could see her starting to come to the realization of what Payton was saying was true. "Are you saying I'm a bad judge of character and that I've also misjudged you? You've asked me to put my life in your hands and I don't have a chance to make it through the night without you."

"Yes."

"Do I have a choice?"

"No."

Marisa put her hand on her stomach. "I think I'm going to be sick."

"My meeting with your husband in the den the other night was not our first. He first tried to have you killed in a car accident that was to be made to look like a gang retaliation because of the story you were investigating."

"How did you know about car accident?"

"Just like I know a lot of things about you. It was no accident."

Marisa's mind began to flash over all the events over the last year in her head, "It was you? Are you telling me it was you?"

Payton didn't answer right away. The pain in his eyes said it all and he bet everything he loved about Marisa on the truth. "Big or small, everything has a price, and the jobs I take have a purpose."

Payton had finished getting ready and checked the clip in his Beretta was full and sent it home. "We have to be out of here early so try to get some rest."

"Where are you going?"

"I need to take a closer look at that gas station of yours." Payton headed for the door.

"What happens in the morning?"

Payton hesitated at the door but didn't turn around. He left and closed the door behind him. Marisa looked into the open duffle bag and saw the deed, a strip of money, the pager, and second Beretta with the silencer attached.

The pager began to beep.

It read: *338546*.

Marisa picked up the gun.

## Chapter 19

Payton's intuition was right. This garage was more than your run of the mill chop shop, it was a hub in the wheel of Westmore's coke delivery system. That is why Westmore had it in his wife's name, waiting for the day he needed his guys on the force to bust it and land her in jail if he needed to get her out of the way in a hurry. Payton was watching one of the attendants restocking the shelves inside the small lobby of the mart keeping up appearances as a legit place of business. It didn't take long before Payton saw a car and a van drive into the station's lot and head toward the oil change bay of the garage. Payton watched through his binoculars as Freddy, the attendant, came out of the mart and slapped his hand on the bay door. The doors opened up in the time it took for the men to get out of their cars and enter the bay, Payton saw what appeared to be a body `strapped up to the back of a tow truck just as the bay doors were closed. Payton then saw the bright lights of the work bay cut back to one set of lights giving the appearance the garage was closed so he stepped from his car into the night air for a closer look.

Wearing his favorite ball cap and a light jacket to try to blend in as best he could in the neighborhood, Payton made his way up the sidewalk on the opposite side of the street and looked and pretended to do a little window shopping. He used the display window as a mirror to keep an eye on the garage and to get a better look around before he decided it was safe enough to get a closer look. There didn't seem to be anyone else coming so Payton made his way down the block a bit before he doubled back on the other side of the street. From his position, he couldn't see inside which meant they couldn't see him so he took a look around. Payton walked up the drive that separated the garage from the cinder block wall that acted as a barrier from the strip mall next door. Payton made his way to the bay window of the bay door and took a peek in. He saw Freddy, Tony, and one of Westmore's body guards standing next to a fourth man he couldn't make out. From his position all he saw was the man wore a hat. Unable to see the man's face, Payton did recognize his voice even though the bay doors had muffled it a bit. The man was talking to a fifth man who was back in the shadows of the poorly lit work station, out of Payton's view.

Payton was right. Inside the working bay of the station was a tow truck that was parked over the opening of the floor, as if it needed an oil change. But by the looks of it, that wasn't the case. There was a man strapped to the back of the tow truck, arms outstretched across the metal frame of the self-loader that was in the up position and feet tied together at the bottom as if he was being sacrificed on a cross. The man's face was already battered and bruised as if he had put up a pretty good fight but had lost. As he spit out a spat of blood from being clocked with a right cross, his blood hit the floor and Robert's shoe. Robert cracked up another right cross and caught the man's jaw flush. This time the man spit out a tooth.

Robert knew the man had to be made an example of for losing a recent shipment. It was a loss Robert could live with but even a small loss couldn't be tolerated. Robert leaned in to the half comatose man and said, "I can't have my shipments being precise month after month then all off a sudden coming up short on your watch, Mr. Torres. That's not good business so I hope you understand, this too, is only business."

Robert pulled on the air hose that hung from the ceiling and uncoiled it as far as it would go before he wrapped it around Torres' neck, then nodded to Freddy who then hit the hydrologic lever that engaged the arms of the self-loader to rotate from the upright position to the loading position. Torres then began to scream but it didn't last long as the slack in the hose quickly cut off his air as it began squeezing the life out of him. Freddy did not stop the hydraulics until Torres' body was almost parallel to the ground.

Robert knew he had Tony's undivided attention. "Tony, I want you to drive to the warehouse tonight. Once there, you will find a truck and a man guarding that truck. Let him know he is to return here right away."

Tony looked over and saw Torres's body give one last effort before succumbing to death. Tony replied but it was a bit off as he was feeling as if he too was out of breath, "Yes, Sir."

"Mia will be a few minutes behind you and bringing further instructions and enough gear to get our operations in Vegas underway and earning."

Robert motioned to Freddy. "Open the doors. Let's get Tony on his way, shall we."

Freddy opened the second set of bay doors so the large repainted U-Haul moving van could exit the garage. No one noticed Payton as he quickly ducked around to the side of the building. Tony climbed into the van and backed out of the garage without saying a word. The fifth man emerged from the shadows and with him, his bodyguard. The man was wearing a business suit, he was not wearing his usual military uniform with the General's insignia on the shoulders. Delgado made his presence known without any words but now he had something to say, "If you lose another one of my shipments again...I don't care if you are family, I'll be making an example out of you next."

Payton had moved down the side wall and now watched from a side door. Payton stepped away from the window and stepped into a small patch of oil that has leaked from an old drum barrel. His foot slid into the drum making a loud thud.

Robert motioned to Delgado's bodyguard to check out the noise. The guard didn't move. Then Delgado himself made a slight gesture and the guard went to take a look.

The bodyguard passed by the side window of the garage. He saw footprints tracking from the oil from only one shoe that led around the back corner of the building. He followed the prints and stopped just before the end of the building to check behind him. Next, he looked around the corner but didn't see anyone. What he did see was the front tip of one of Payton's shoes that stuck out from beyond the end of the dumpster on the far side. The bodyguard drew his weapon and slowly continued toward the dumpster. He glanced inside the dumpster but didn't see anything other than empty boxes and Styrofoam peanuts. He looked back down at the shoe then adjusted his weight like a cat ready to pounce. Suddenly, the bodyguard found himself caught in a pair of headlights from a car that was coming right at him. The bodyguard turned into the direction of the car to get a good look at the driver, and now had his back to the dumpster. The guard took aim with his weapon at the driver's side of the windshield. The car skidded to a halt twenty feet from the bodyguard just as he was getting ready to fire. At that moment, Payton popped out of the dumpster and pistol whipped the bodyguard out cold. Marisa stepped from the car with the Beretta Payton had left for her in hand.

"Get back in the car," Payton said with as much urgency as he could without making too much noise as he jumped from the dumpster and grabbed his shoe from the ground he had used as a decoy. All Marisa saw was a man with a gun emerge from around the corner of the building to shoot at Payton. Marisa fired a shot in the direction of the man who appeared to look a lot like the silhouette she had been using in Payton's basement firing range. Her shot missed her target hitting the building sending a ricochet that glanced off the man's shoulder. The man ducked behind the corner of the building for cover.

Payton dashed for the car and climbed in on the passenger side. Marisa was already behind the wheel and backed the car onto the street, changed gears, and sped off.

Marisa was driving and everything about her was shaking. She still held the gun her hand as she drove.

Payton took the gun from her. "It's easier to drive without this."

"Who was that?"

"That was your husband."

"Oh shit."

"Yeah, that about sums it up. By the way, whose car is this, and why aren't you back at the hotel in bed?

"Not to worry. I rented the car with the cash from the bag and is that really where you want me right now?

"We'll have to go back and continue this conversation some other time. What I want right now is for you to turn the car around and head back the other way."

"I thought the hotel was in this direction?"

"It is," Payton pointed behind them, "but the money is going in that direction."

≠

Westmore was with Freddy in front of the station, "After we leave, I want this station and everything in it, burned to the ground....and make it obvious it was arson"

"Won't that draw the police on us?"

"No. They'll be looking for the owner of the station—my wife."

Payton and Marisa sat in the rental car parked some 20 miles north of the city, just off Highway 15 that led the fallen from the city of angels toward Las Vegas.

Payton looked at Marisa and was glad she was there next to him but at the same time, she was too close. "Why didn't you stay in the hotel?"

Marisa hands the pager to Payton. "After you left, the pager went off again. Don't you have a cell phone?"

"Yes, I do, but sometimes I prefer low tech. It's too easy to trace cell phones these days."

Payton looked at the number on the pager: 338546. "You know what this means, don't you?"

"It means what I have been feeling is true."

"What's that?"

"When I saw Mia's number on the pager I felt something I never felt before." Marisa looked in Payton's eyes and tried to see if her words would be able to touch his humanity or if his chosen path had walled up his heart completely. She knew better, she felt their time together was real and not just going through the motions. "As much as I love my family, I can only picture them right now...I can't feel them. I feel as if I can't trust anyone right now."

"Consider that reality a blessing. It's going to keep you alive."

The pager goes off. 338546. Devlin.

"I've made myself a promise that when this is over and we are both still alive..."

"Yes?"

"I want my own on-line erotic magazine and photography studio. No more crime scenes. No more trying to capture the finality of death. Somewhere I can work with other photographers from around the world sharing ideas and portraits celebrating the sensuality we all desire."

"I hope you can keep that promise." Payton watched as the van driven by Tony passed their position. "It's time."

"Time for what?"

"Everything you've done up until now has been legal. What we are about to do breaks all the rules."

All Marisa can do is nod.

≠

Robert Westmore was standing in an old barn style warehouse as he spoke with Mia on the phone. "You heard me, she's not dead." Robert took a look around the 4000 square foot abandoned hay loft. "I don't know where they are. Take care of Tony then finish this once and for all...kill them both."

# Chapter 20

Marisa followed a few hundred yards behind the van driven by Tony, trying to keep the headlights from drawing any unwanted attention. Payton was in the back seat going over the plan one more time. "Remember, just before we pass the van, turn on the interior light and look at that envelope as if you are looking at a set of directions. Make sure your blouse is open enough, we want to get his attention."

"How about I just take off my bra while I'm at it? You better duck down or he's going to see more than just my tits."

$$\neq$$

Tony had just finished eating his New York sub and tossed the used wrapper behind him through the open doorway that led into the back of the van. The smell of the old tires filling the back didn't help the taste of his sandwich. The stench wasn't going away even with the windows down so Tony lit up a cigarette and tossed the match out the window into the dry desert air. He looked over to the left as Marisa passed his van. He stayed in the slow lane and double checked to make sure he stayed under the speed limit as he saw the interior light come on in Marisa's car. Marisa turned her body a bit in Tony's direction as she leaned toward the passenger side as she picked up the envelope from the seat. Tony got what they wanted—an eye full of Marisa as she looked up at Tony watching her and gave him a slight smile. Marisa turned off the light then sped up on ahead.

A few minutes down the road Tony saw Marisa's rental car on the side of the road, parked near a small drainage ditch. The hood of the car was up. Tony slowed down, passed the car, and pulled over to help.

Tony shut off the engine, took the keys, and locked the van before he went back to see if he could help the lovely stranded motorist. "Is everything okay? Is there something I could do to help?"

Payton had made his way up out of the shadows of the drainage ditch and walked up behind Tony and as he did, he put the end of the barrel of his Beretta to Tony's ribs. "What you can do, is to decide to live...or die."

"I just stopped to help. What's going on? Who are you?"

"My name is Clyde...This here is Bonnie. I'll tell you what, you help us and I'll help you to see tomorrow."

Marisa reached out and with a bit of confidence took the keys for the van from Tony. "How about we trade our car for your van?"

Payton leaned in, pressing the gun a little firmer to Tony's ribs. "If you can do that for us we won't mention it to your boss, Delgado, we let you go."

"So it sounds like you know who you're stealing from and there's no way I can get far enough away, unless you throw in a set of new tires with trade."

Payton thought about it. "I'll tell you what, I'll throw in a spare as well if you show us on the map where the warehouse is."

Marisa handed over the keys to the car to Tony. "That sounds like a pretty sweet deal, Tony. I'll tell you what, forget the spare. Let's make it two sets of tires. How about it, Tony?"

$$\neq$$

The 12 foot moving van was headed back down the highway toward Los Angeles. Payton was driving and still shaking his head, "Do you know how much money you just gave him?"

"What's a set of tires go for these days, four hundred dollars?"

"Let me tell you a little about your gas station. It's quite a slick operation. A call comes in for a buy, a tow truck responds to the scene, and the switch is made. Right out in the open."

"Switch?"

"Yeah, the switch. The buyer places the money in the tire and when the truck responds and changes the flat, the deal is made."

Marisa was afraid to ask but she did anyway, "What's inside the other tire?"

"Let's say to keep the orders simple, probably one kilo per tire."

"Are you telling me we are driving around in a van full of cocaine?"

"Actually, we are in a van full of the profits. Tony was probably on his way to one of their drop sites to add this load to a larger truck before taking it on to Vegas to have it washed through some sort of holding company. I'm sure Robert has a connection with one or more businesses to launder the money through."

"Real estate. I heard him talking about some real estate deals in Las Vegas."

"Okay, real estate. Maybe he makes a few quick sweetheart deals to make a quick sale, taking a small loss but that's the price of business."

"And banks. I'm pretty sure he mentioned a couple of banks in there too."

"If he uses the banks, he has to keep the deposits under 10 grand per day to avoid the I.R.S., then over a month he can draw it out to make his property sales, thereby turning the money over a couple of times and it comes out clean on the other side."

"Can we go back a minute? That means my name is on the deed to a coke lab."

"You mean the garage? No, that was a distribution center. The lab is going to be someplace a little more remote."

"I think I'm going to be sick."

"Keep it together, Marisa. We still have a lot of work to do."

"We've got the van. Let's just go. You can start over. We can find your family."

"No!"

Marisa is taken back by Payton's steadfast answer and doesn't understand, "We have enough money right here to find them and for you to start your life over."

"Why would I want to do it all over again? Everything I've done has led me to here and now you are safe."

Marisa realized Payton just admitted his whole life has led up to this moment, and her. No one had ever made her feel that wanted, ever.

Payton took her silence as she understood. "It's not about the resources to find them...it's about the resources to keep them alive. I'm going to have to kill your husband to do that. Are you going to have a problem with that?"

Marisa rolled down the window and vomited outside the van. Payton pulled the van over and stopped on the side of the road.

On the side of the road next to the van, Marisa was bent over from just vomiting. The night's cool, desert air was evident by the fact you could see Marisa's breath as she seemed to be exhausted physically as well as emotionally. Payton found a rag in the glove box and handed it to Marisa to wipe her mouth. "Are you going to be okay? Are you sick?"

"No. I'm pregnant."

Payton knew it wasn't his but in the back of his mind, he wished it was. "I'm going after them, and in order to keep my promise, I'm going to have to kill them all. Are you okay with that?"

"What does that make me if I say, yes? Would that make you feel better about what you do?"

Payton didn't want to give Marisa the real answer that he was doing it for her, he just said, "You don't deserve this," and walked around the front of the van, climbing in behind the wheel. Marisa went up to the passenger side window.

Payton did his best to hide his emotions. "This is going to be my only chance to catch them off guard. I feel I have to go do this, and if I fail, I don't want you anywhere around. I want you long gone."

Marisa knew as well as Payton he was right. This was his world, not hers. But at the same time, his heart didn't want to let her go, it felt wrong.

Marisa's plea hit a chord with Payton, "You said you wouldn't leave me."

Payton closed his eyes as if to pray for an answer. The only thing that came to him was, "*What if this was the last time he would ever see her?*"

## Chapter 21

Marisa slowly opened the passenger door to the van and climbed in, trying not to make any noise, almost as if Payton didn't hear her, he wouldn't notice. Of course every squeak and clank of the old truck door seemed to be amplified. The click of the handle, the rusty hinges whining from the weight of the loose door as it swung open and then back again, to the gentle click as Marisa pulled the door shut to a close.

The whole time Marisa was trying to be stealthy and get back into the truck, Payton rested his head down on his folded arms across the top of the steering wheel. He closed his eyes trying to fight back his feelings for Marisa and he knew the logical thing to do would be to let her go but his heart was telling him otherwise.

"Payton, the only thing I have to believe in is your word."

Payton opened his eyes and looked to Marisa. "Do I have yours?"

Marisa looked at Payton in a way he already knew the answer. He saw it in her eyes. She had already given herself and her trust over to him and now it was up to Payton to keep her alive.

Payton handed Marisa the small map with a few instructions on it they got from Freddy. "Take this. We're not too far from that exit on that map."

"Exit 64. U.S. 93."

"Yeah, 64. I think they'd have a drop location out that way and that's possibly where Tony was headed."

"Drop what?"

Suddenly, the front windshield was pierced by a high-caliber bullet. The shot passed through the tempered glass and lodged into the back of the worn out bench seat between them.

"Get down!" Payton grabbed Marisa's shoulder and pulled her down to the seat as she slipped as low as she could to the flooring.

Payton started the van and sped off down the highway and as he did, he saw Mia across the highway climbing back into a large tank like Hummer. As she did, she laid her rifle down as not to damage the high-powered scope. Mia then crossed over the median and was in pursuit of Payton and Marisa as they tried to get a lead off down the highway.

Marisa still had her head down. "Who's shooting at us now?"

"It's Mia. Something's not right, she doesn't usually miss and that is twice now.

Marisa cautiously crawled up into the passenger seat. "None of this is right."

Another shot from Mia hit the van. Payton shoved Marisa head down. "Keep your head down. I don't know if we can out run her in this van."

Marisa had her head down between her legs. She saw a faint red glow coming from under the seat. She reached under and carefully pulled out an old red grease monkey's towel that was covering the digital clock of a bomb. "I don't think Tony was intended to make it to Las Vegas."

"What makes you say that?"

Marisa quickly sat up. "What does a bomb look like?"

"A block of clay or like red flares, some wires, and with some sort of timing device attached to it, why?"

"I thinks there's one under my seat."

"Is it armed?"

"How am I supposed to know?"

"Look to see if there is a light on."

Marisa took a look as another shot from Mia hit the van. Marisa sprang back up again.

"There are two lights, both are off."

"Is there a timer?"

"A red clock...yes."

"What does it read?"

Marisa takes another look. "Ten minutes."

"No problem."

Marisa popped back up. "No problem! Hey, I'm the one sitting on the damn thing! I'm getting in back."

Marisa started to climb into the back of the van.

"You don't want to go back there."

Marisa was already in back before he can finish. "Gross!"

Marisa climbed back into the front passenger seat. "There's a dead woman back there wrapped in cellophane like a mummy.

Payton had seen Sorina's body back there but didn't want to freak Marisa out anymore by telling her. "Are you telling me you would rather sit on a bomb than sit next to a corpse?"

"I think I'm going to be sick again."

Marisa put her head down between her legs. She was looking at the bomb when she saw the red power indicator light come on.

"Oh my God."

"Are you going to be okay, Marisa?"

"The red light just came on."

"What about the other light? What color is it?"

"It looks to be green."

"Is it on?"

"No."

"That's good. That means the timer is not activated."

Marisa sat back up in her seat. "The green light just came on!"

Payton checked his rearview mirror. Mia was gaining ground on the van.

"Mia must have a remote of some kind."

"Check to see if the timer is running."

Marisa checked the bomb then sat back up. "No."

Payton began to think out loud as he often did, "What is she waiting for?"

"I think we're coming up on exit 64."

"Check the timer."

Marisa checked the timer. She was about to sit back up when the green light started to flash and the timer started to count down.

10...9...

Marisa quickly back up and was frantic. "It's not 10 minutes, it's seconds, and it's running."

"Pull a wire!"

Marisa ducked back down to check the bomb.

6...5...

"Pull one. Any one!"

Marisa pulled a wire of the clip from the micro switch. The clock stopped...at 3.

"It stopped."

"Okay. Now tell me what does it look like?

"It looks like a block of modeling clay about half the size of a cube of butter."

"That's plastic explosive and enough to blow the doors off this van and incinerate everything inside, which I assume was the intention."

"Intention?"

"To leave two unidentified bodies and enough evidence to keep the police busy while they get away with a bigger payload. Now make sure the wire from the timer doesn't touch any metal."

Marisa stuck the end of the wire into the block of C-4 itself, then sat up.

"Is it hot in here or is it just me?"

Payton could see the Marisa's face was red from being bent over for too long as the blood had rushed to her head. "I think you better roll down the window and get some air."

Mia checked the remote detonator. The red power indicator was lit but the green activation light had gone out. She tried the toggle switch to no avail. Mia left the toggle in the "on" position then dropped the trigger onto the passenger seat. Mia's next move was to try to pass Payton on the left but Payton maneuvered to cut her off. Mia then backed off and tried to pass on the right. She was coming up alongside the van when the windshield of her Hummer was greeted by a massive splat of vomit. Mia was forced to slow down and pull in behind the van. She hit the wipers and cleared most of it off only to see the van pulling away.

Marisa leaned back in from the window and wiped her mouth with the towel.

Payton took a look in the side review mirror and saw the Hummer's lights getting closer. "It's not over yet."

"No, I think I'm done."

"No, what I'm saying is, Mia is still on our tail."

"Can we out run her?"

"I've been running for years...you wouldn't like it."

"If I don't get the chance, I just wanted to thank you for saving my life."

Payton looked at Marisa and smiled and thought, "No, you saved mine," but instead decided to tell her, "You're welcome. Thank you for letting me." They both smiled and then Payton added, "Are you ready?"

Marisa tightened her seat belt then returned a scared but confident look.

Payton let off the gas and slowed the van a bit. "Be ready for anything and hang on tight." Payton then hit the brakes hard and brought the van to a quick stop.

Mia had floored the Hummer and was trying to catch the van and her actions played right into Payton's hands. The Hummer was far behind when Mia saw the brakes lights come on and van skidding to a stop causing Mia to put her vehicle into a skid. Mia whipped the wheel to avid slamming into the back of the van and in doing so put Hummer into a ninety degree sliding stop just short of the van.

Payton put the van in reverse. "Hang on."

"What are you doing?"

"I'm pissing her off. She'll be more predictable that way."

"Great."

Payton nodded to Marisa then hit the gas.

Mia was in the process of reaching for the detonator that had been knocked to the floor when she heard the tires on the van start to squeal and saw the van was coming back at her very quickly.

Mia ducked in between the seats as the van's impact shattered her side windows on the Hummer sending broken glass all over the inside and all over her.

Payton was changing gears as Marisa was regrouping in her seat belt. "Do you think she is pissed off yet?"

"She's getting there."

Mia sat up and shook the glass off of her. As Mia watched the van drive away, she began to pick the glass out of her hair. With one final shake, Mia put the Hummer back in gear to continue her pursuit.

# Chapter 22

Payton was driving as fast as the converted moving van could go. Marisa had the map with the instructions in hand when she saw the highway sign for U.S. 95 was one mile ahead. "Okay, it's the next exit."

Payton knew this van couldn't out run Mia in the Hummer but if they could get off the main highway, they might have a chance to pull off and get the van out of sight. Payton took the exit 64 off ramp, turned left, and cut under the overpass.

Payton was speeding along and in control and was finally able to take a breath thinking they might have a chance now. Marisa continued to go over the instructions.

"Where did Tony say the warehouse was?"

"It's not far from here."

Payton was trying get as much distance as he could between him and Mia as he took a look back to see if Mia had followed them off the highway. He wasn't sure if it was her but a set of headlights pulled off the same ramp as they had just used. Marisa took a peek up over the edge of the map to try to find the next turn but it was difficult with the poor lighting. "Watch it, tracks!"

It was too late. Payton crossed the railroad tracks at full speed. The loose wire on the bomb under Marisa's seat shook free from the C-4 plastic explosive.

Payton just made the signal as the traffic began to move in the other direction. Mia had to slow her Hummer as she got caught behind a flat-bed truck at the red light. The flat-bed took a right on the red then once the truck had cleared, Mia ran the light through the intersection.

Payton drove the van as best he could down the old road trying to avoid the potholes. Each time he hit one, he could feel the weight of the load of tires shift enough to make the van sway as if in a strong wind. There was an old sign ahead for a salvage yard and when they reached it, it looked like it was closed. As he drove past he saw an old rusty crane that was nothing but the track base and the cab parked beside the large white cinder block wall that made up the south side of the yard's border, the long arm had been removed probably for scrap metal.

It wasn't long before Mia passed the salvage yard. She felt the heavy duty tires of the Hummer growling on the battered pavement beneath her. A she passed the end of the yard, she was so focused on gaining ground, she didn't realize Payton had pulled off and parked the white moving van behind an old crane just beyond the side yard, using the white brick wall as camouflage.

≠

Payton chambered a round in the Beretta and offered the gun to Marisa. She shook him off. "Do you think she saw us?"

"No, if she had, she would have done something right then."

Payton waited a few minutes then followed Mia at a safe distance with the headlights off assuming she was headed to the same destination as they had on their map. Payton drove the van onto an old road which was marked with plenty of potholes. The van took a good jolt from a deep hole that shook Marisa pretty good. "I think you might have missed a few. You want to go back and get them too?"

Payton took the joke lightly because it made him think Marisa was feeling safe with him even though he didn't show it. He could see the back of Hummer as Mia tapped the brakes as she avoided the holes. The loose wire on the bomb swayed with each bump, then on the next good hit, the end if the wire made contact with the metal seat frame for just an instant. The indicator light flashed and the timer clicked down— 2 seconds remained on the digital clock.

Mia drove up to an empty three story warehouse. Its old wooden frame and rusty metal patchwork gave the word "gloomy" new meaning. Mia got out of her beast of a vehicle and saw the doors were still padlocked. She went back to the Hummer and pulled the tire iron from the encased jack set, broke open the lock, and flung open the main twin barn doors that led into the warehouse.

Once inside, Mia threw the main power switch to light up the inside of the warehouse. A 24 foot moving truck sat parked in the open lobby. Mia walked over to the back of the truck and used the crow bar to pry off the lock on the back of the truck. Mia chucked the old lock, flipped the safety catch, rolled over the lever releasing the door, and rolled it up exposing a truck full of tires.

Mia couldn't help but talk to herself, "That looks like a lot more than five million dollars. Closer to ten."

≠

Payton had stopped the van just up the road from the warehouse. He checked the clip from his gun then sent it back home.

"This is as far as you go."

"Is it the money?"

"If it was...you'd be dead by now."

"Gee, I think that's the nicest thing you've said to me."

Payton climbed out of the van and closed the door. Marisa moved over into the driver's seat.

"There's enough tires back there that are worth about twenty-five grand a piece. You're looking at about a million and a half of dirty money. Invest it in property then turn it quickly at a good price and after commission, you might end up about a million. That should be enough to start your studio and be far enough away from this mess. After tonight, I don't think anyone will be looking for you."

"What about Robert?"

"I'm sure he's on his way. You better get on your way, too." Payton felt he was sending away the best thing that had ever happened to him but it would be ever harder on him if he got her killed, all for naught. "Don't forget to ditch the van. You're carrying dead weight, remember?"

Payton started to walk toward the warehouse.

"You don't have to do this," Marisa pleaded.

Payton stopped and looked back. They exchange parting glances then Payton nodded good bye. "Yes, I do."

Payton turned back to the warehouse with fire and determination growing in his eyes. He pulled back on the slide of his gun and cleared the existing round for a new one. The round flipped into the air and Payton caught it, as he did every time, and put the live round in his pocket. Marisa saw this and was reminded of the round she found lying on her bedroom landing. For the first time Marisa saw herself as a "The Mark."

≠

Mia pried open the office filing cabinets. Files were tossed all around the office like a ticker tape parade. One of the files was marked "Personal Property."

In one of the drawers, Mia came across a short stack of DVDs bundled together labeled "Assets." She tossed them over her shoulder. The discs hit a free hanging light that hung from the ceiling that sent it in a freewheeling motion that caused shadows to dance chaotic all over the room.

As Marisa drove away down the old road, the right front headlight was loose and rattled to the tempo of the bumpy road. The loose wire on the bomb swayed freely as it pleased. Marisa was coming up on the salvage yard and in the distance she could see a set of headlights coming in her direction. Marisa turned off her headlights, pulled off the road, and parked the van once again behind the old crane. She watched the truck pass but didn't recognize the driver.

As Freddy drove the old road, he hit a pothole and knocked the rear view mirror loose. Freddy reset the mirror and as he did, he took a glance at the back of the truck filled with gas cans.

Payton could hear the rumble of Freddy's truck approaching. He took a look back down the road and realized he hadn't been seen so he quickly ducked inside the warehouse and hid behind a stack of 55 gallon drums. From behind the drums Payton could hear Freddy brake the truck to a squealing stop.

Mia heard the same sound. She had been expecting Freddy but just in case she turned out the office light and took cover in the dark.

Freddy saw the doors open and assumed it was Tony who had left them that way. He entered carrying a 5 gallon gas can in each hand, full of fuel for the generator. He walked over to the open doors on the moving truck. He knew what was supposed to be in the truck but hadn't opened it on his boss's orders. Freddy dropped the cans in disbelief. His mind was racing trying to calculate the maximum capacity of the truck and how many tires it could hold. All his mind could come up to say was, "There is a God."

Freddy grabbed one of the tires and pulled it out far enough that he could get his hand inside and feel around. He felt a block of something about the size of a small shoe box. He pulled it out and saw he was holding a stack of cash that was wrapped in cellophane. He put it to his face and smelled it like it was the best piece of chocolate cake he had his hands on. He then slipped it back in the tire and closed the drop down door, latching it secure. Freddy did a fist pump like he just scored a touchdown and in all of the excitement didn't notice that Payton watched him from behind the barrels. Freddy climbed into the cab of the truck, saw the keys, and pulled them from the ignition then dropped them in his pocket. A he turned around, there was Payton with his Beretta trained on Freddy.

"How would you like to meet your God, up close, and personal?" Payton's sarcastic comment caught Freddy off guard.

That's when it hit Freddy, he had forgotten the golden rule, "don't count your chickens before they hatch." In this case, "don't count your tires before you launder their contents." "Go to hell."

"I hear the weather in Hellville is not so great this time of year. You will send me a post card, won't you?"

Freddy's eyes darted a look over Payton's shoulder. Payton didn't miss the uncontrollable glance from Freddy. Payton knew it could only be one other person coming up behind him. Mia.

Mia took a two handed grip on the tire iron like it was a baseball bat and was about to take a swing when out of nowhere came, "Look out, Payton!" It was Marisa. She had doubled back when she had seen Freddy's truck pulling up to the warehouse. She stood at the entrance of the lobby with the Beretta Payton had given her. She was aiming in the direction of all three of them when she realized if she fired, she might hit Payton and lowered the gun.

Mia caught this and coiled the tire iron and was about to follow through when Payton grabbed Freddy, spun him around, and put Freddy between him and Mia. Mia swung the tire iron so fiercely, it lodged right in the middle of Freddy's chest with a vengeance. With Freddy still in Payton's arms and agonizing in pain from the tire iron sticking out of his chest, Payton and Mia each drew their Berettas at the same time and fired. Payton had shot Mia in the chest, knowing she was wearing a bullet proof vest, knocking her to the ground. Mia's round struck Freddy in the chest killing him instantly. As Mia fell back and hit the ground, she dropped her gun out of reach.

Freddy had become dead weight in Payton's arms. Payton stood Freddy's corpse up against the side of the truck to find the keys to the van in Freddy's pocket.

Mia regained control of most of her senses and went for her gun. She grabbed the gun and whirled to shoot Payton, but instead shot Freddy's corpse that was still leaning up against the truck. Freddy's body fell and spun to the ground with a loud thud. The crowbar was still in his chest.

# Chapter 23

Payton tried to start the truck but the engine was cold. He pumped the accelerator a couple of times then tried the keys once more. The engine fluttered but did not start. This time, Payton pumped the accelerator and on the third pump held it to the floor as he turned the key and the engine began to sputter, then cough, then finally roared to life. Payton heard a tap on the passenger side window that got his attention. It was Mia tapping the end of her Beretta that she now had pointed at Payton. Mia waived her left hand a couple of times across her throat indicating to Payton she wanted him to kill the engine and he did.

Mia was now the one giving the orders. "Let's go find your Marisa."

Mia led Payton by gun point to the middle of the warehouse. "Call to her."

"Marisa!" Payton knew she was still nearby. "Run!"

Mia kneed Payton in the back of his leg making him fall to his knees.

"He's dead! Can you hear me? If you don't come out right now, he's dead!"

Marisa had found Payton's hiding place back behind the 55 gallon drums near the entrance of the warehouse. Through a small gap in the barrels, she could see Mia had her gun to the back of Payton's head. It occurred to Marisa, she couldn't win. How do you outthink a psychopath? Marisa cautiously stepped out from behind the barrels into plain view.

Mia focused the end of Beretta on Payton and made sure Marisa could see she had her finger on the trigger. "Come here."

Marisa started to come forward but Payton didn't want her any closer. "Stay there."

Marisa stopped in her tracks. Mia wasn't up for any games and whipped Payton upside the head with the butt of the Beretta just hard enough to get both of their attention but not enough to knock him out.

Again Mia made her request known, "Come. Here."

Payton shook his head "no" to Marisa and she stayed where she was.

Mia tried a different tactic. "Do you know why you're doing this? You can bet he does," Mia paused waiting for an answer she knew would never come, "he did it for me."

Marisa had known they had once been a team but didn't know how close they really were. "Maybe that is true but I also know it doesn't matter now, does it?"

"You guess?" Marisa had tried to hurt Mia but instead had made it clear what she had long felt—she didn't feel anything. She didn't feel the love she once felt for Payton nor the hate she should have for Delgado for making her this away. Someplace between her heart and her mind she thought she might shed a tear but that would mean she cared, and right now, right here, she had nothing left. "Tell me what I want to know. Now."

Marisa was torn between running and wanting to stay and help the man who saved her life. "I..."

Payton again shook his head "no." He knew if Marisa gave Mia the information, they were both as good as dead. Marisa gave Payton a little smile that was more out of fear. "Payton is a great photographer. Did you know that? I was thinking about hiring him myself."

Mia found this quip to be quite humorous and got a little chuckle out of it, Payton too. But Mia wasn't ready to waste any more time. "Yes, that is true. You should see the ones he's been taking of you over the last eight months. Some of them are downright tastefully...personal?"

"I have," Marisa had lied. She had thought Payton had only had her under surveillance over the last couple of months, at least that was the impression Payton had given her, but didn't want Mia to think otherwise.

Mia gave back a little smile of her own. "It's too bad you two will never know what could have been."

Mia raised her gun in Marisa's direction. From his knees, Payton threw his shoulder into Mia, and knocked her off balance. "Run, Marisa!"

Mia regained her balance, took one step towards Payton and decided to return the favor and shot Payton's center mass of his lightweight bulletproof vest. At that close range, the force sent Payton backwards into the wooden center post, slamming his head hard against it, knocking himself out. Mia turned and took aim at Marisa but she was no longer by the barrels. Out of the corner of her eye, Mia caught a glimpse of Marisa as she ran out through the open front doors, and quickly swung her arm around and fired twice. Both shots missed but the second shot had hit the van that Marisa had parked just up the road not chancing getting any closer without being heard. Mia's mind was spinning. Everything she was with Payton was gone but the emotions that he once suppressed were wanting things back as they once were. But what Delgado had turned her into had not only forced her to accept herself as Mia, but also unlocked the rage she couldn't control any longer.

Mia grabbed one of the gas cans and started to pour gasoline all over the warehouse and as she made her way back to the center of the room, she shook the gas can and heard the swish of the last of the gasoline. Without even thinking about it, she poured the last of it on Payton.

Once Marisa had cleared the doors and was out of the line of sight of Mia, she saw the Hummer and the moving van and took refuge between them on the far side of the Hummer. As Marisa was looking through the cab of the vehicle from the passenger side door, she watched the entrance of the warehouse to see if she was being followed, that's when she saw Mia's lengthy shadow creep out of the entrance ahead of her. Marisa grabbed the side mirror, stepped onto the running board, then sat down below the level of the passenger window out of sight.

Marisa was gripping on the side mirror so tight from all of the adrenaline that was also circulating the fear through her. She thought about what Payton had taught her about controlling her breathing when he taught her how to use the Beretta. She took a deep breath and slowly let it out. Marisa slowly raised her head and took a peek through the passenger window and saw Mia's shadow retreating into the warehouse. That's when she saw the red light of the detonator that was lying on the passenger seat of the Hummer and the light that indicated the power was "on" was lit.

Marisa slowly shifted her weight as not to make any noise as she climbed off of the running board. As quiet as she could, she opened the passenger door, and took the detonator. With a flick of her thumb, she flipped both switches to the "off" position and the indicator light went out.

Marisa then went to the passenger door of the moving van. She knew when she tried to open the door it was going to creak, so as slow as she could, she opened the door. Marisa looked under the passenger seat but it was too dark to see the loose wire to reconnect it. She had to take a chance and activate the power to the bomb in order to see the wire's contact point. She took a deep breath and flicked the power switch. The red lights on both the detonator and the bomb lit up and so did the digital clock that illuminated the face of the clock that indicated, 1 second.

≠

Mia climbed into the cab, went to start it, and realized the keys were missing. She figured Payton must have them and when she checked her side mirror she noticed Payton was gone. She sat there for a couple of minutes listening as best she could to see if Payton would give away his location. She heard nothing but silence so she climbed out of the cab, drew her Beretta, and cautiously made her way down the back end, using the truck for cover she took a look around. She saw Payton's shirt lying on the ground behind the truck. As she picked it up, she could smell the fumes from the gas soaked shirt. Suddenly, from above, she was being doused with gasoline. The fuel pouring over her head took her breath away and caused her to drop her weapon. She started to reach for her gun when she heard Payton's warning, "Don't." She looked up and saw Payton holding a flare and was ready to strike it. "You might want to rethink your next move."

"You might want to rethink yours, too. You strike that, this whole place can go up, and you along with it."

Both Mia and Payton heard the van start up just outside the warehouse and pull away.

Mia shrugged. "Looks like she has made her choice and you weren't it."

Payton felt his heart drop, but he knew in the long run, it was probably the best thing for her. His sadness was short-lived as they heard the roar of the engine get louder and the headlight beams from the van light up the entrance to the warehouse. Mia reached down and grabbed her Beretta and was blinded by the van's headlights that were drawing closer by the second. She stood and got off two rounds at Marisa's silhouette behind the wheel of the van.

The van came to a stop up against the first of three center posts that supported the center arch of the warehouse and in doing so, killed the engine. Upon impact Marisa's body slumped over the steering wheel.

Payton shouted, "Marisa!" Payton dove off the hood tackling Mia to the ground before she could get a shot off. Payton wrestled the Beretta away from Mia. He released the clip and cleared the chamber. Payton staggered to his feet, and emotionally drained, allowed Mia to get up. "Why, Mia?"

"You know why, Payton. It's what we're trained to do. It's who we are."

"You're wrong, she had nothing to do with this. This is about Delgado and it always has been." Payton turned and saw the dark interior of the cab and the silhouette of Marisa's body slumped over the wheel. With what emotional strength he had left, he walked over to her, and as he laid his hand on her shoulder to lean her back he was relieved. Not that she had died quickly from the two shots that were center mass in her chest but that it was not her. Payton noticed the passenger door was open and realized Marisa had put Sorina's dead body behind the wheel and drove the van from the passenger side as she was ducked down below the dash. After hitting the post she had made her escape out the passenger side as Payton had leapt off the hood to tackle Mia.

Payton felt a second wind knowing Marisa was still alive. He saw something move to his right and as he turned saw Marisa standing there. He saw the look on Marisa's face turned from joy to fear just as Payton caught a glance of the block and tackle rig, which hung down from a guide rail that was attached to the ceiling, was swinging at him. Before he could react, the rig slammed into him knocking him into the ground. Payton saw Mia going for the clip that was on the ground he had ejected from the Beretta. The moving van had enough clearance, Payton could crawl under it to the other side, and as he did, he saw Marisa running from the warehouse.

Mia found the clip but not the Beretta. She quickly looked around for something to use as a weapon and all she could find was the crowbar that was still lodged in Freddy's chest.

Just as Payton stood up, Mia slammed the crowbar across Payton's back causing him to stumble in the direction of the freight elevator. The second whack from the crowbar across the backside of his bulletproof vest caused him to stumble and fall into the elevator. Mia joined Payton in the elevator, lowered the gate, and hit the button for the third floor.

Just as the elevator began to move, so did Payton. He stood, weakened by Mia, but not by the loss he felt for Marisa. Mia tried to take another swing at Payton but he was able to block it, and eventually get the crowbar away from her. But when he whirled it at her, he lost his grip and the crowbar hit the wall and then the floor. As he went to reach for it, Mia kicked it across the elevator floor and it slid through the bottom of the gate and out. When it hit the lobby floor it rattled around and stopped at the feet of Marisa who had returned with the Beretta Payton had dropped and the clip. Payton saw her load the gun and she was ready to use it when he hollered, "Marisa, go, take the van and go!"

About a hundred yards from the warehouse, Robert Westmore had stopped his car and was walking up the road toward the warehouse when he saw a moving van back out of the warehouse and stop.

Inside the van, Marisa sat and tried to make sense of everything, but nothing made sense. She looked over and saw the detonator lying in the passenger seat.

Robert saw the driver's door of the van open and, to his surprise, watched Marisa climb out and walk back towards the entrance to the warehouse with what looked like a gun in her hand.

≠

The elevator had stopped on the third floor but the intensity of the fight had not. Payton was able to thrust an elbow into Mia's side which sent both of them flying to the back of the elevator. They both hit the back wall hard and they both decided to swing in opposite directions in order to catch their breath. Payton lifted the gate and gestured to Mia she may exit first. Mia countered with the same. As Payton walked out, Mia hit the down button on the elevator and lowered the gate and she walked out sending the elevator down to the first floor. Mia reached under her jacket and pulled out a knife. Payton countered with the same.

Mia knew one of them was not going to leave this place alive. "Prepare to meet your maker."

"God has nothing to do with this."

The knife blades shimmered as the two wheeled and dealed. Mia sliced Payton's shirt open and exposed his vest. "Is that a new vest?"

"Yeah, you like it?"

"I guess I'm going to have to kill you for it."

"I guess you must not want it very badly then."

The fight was back on. Mia caught the back of Payton's hand forcing him to drop his knife. "Lookie there. Now what? I have a knife..." Mia reached in her jacket and pulled out a Beretta from the other side of her double holster, "...and a gun."

Payton knew what he wanted, "I'll take the gun."

"How about I give you the knife?"

Mia put the gun in the small of her back and then started to wheel the knife at Payton. As Payton began to back track, he grabbed anything he could get his hands on to protect himself—books, files, even a chair. Then he finally grabbed onto a free standing lamp. The five foot light stand worked great as a staff to ward off Mia's advance. Mia drew her Beretta causing Payton to back his way to the open wall at the edge of the floor, which fell off into the lobby of the warehouse. Payton looked down to the entrance of the building where Marisa was standing. They made eye contact and Marisa took a few steps in closer. That was when Payton saw Robert Westmore, The Jaguar, walking up behind Marisa and she was completely unaware.

# Chapter 24

From the 20 feet above, Payton stood on the edge of the flooring and as he saw Robert was quickly approaching Marisa from behind. "Marisa, look out!"

At that same moment, Robert grabbed Marisa from behind in a bear hug. Her arms were instantly pinned to her side. Pinning the Beretta that was clenched in her right hand to her body.

Robert's voice could have not been more of an unwelcomed surprise. "I love the way your body quivers when you are in my arms."

"Yeah, well it looks like I quivered one too many times. I'm pregnant."

Robert acts like he doesn't care but it does get him where it hurts, in his black heart. He tries to play it off. "Hey, Payton? Do you think I'll make a good father?"

"You don't know what love is. How could you make a good father?"

"Are you sure it's even mine? Mia tells me you and Payton have gotten real close."

"Hey, Payton, I guess the deal's off since I'm going to have to be the one to do your job for you."

Marisa ground her teeth as she gripped the Beretta hoping to have the chance to use it. "You're a bastard."

"Yes, I am." Robert changed his attention back to the upper floor. "Hey, Mia!"

Mia walked into view at the edge of the open wall near Payton. At this point neither Payton nor Mia seemed to care about killing each other but did mind what they saw below. Mia finally noticed what Payton knew all along, even though Robert had control of Marisa, Marisa had control of the detonator in her left hand.

Marisa looked at Payton and for the first time, Payton saw she was willing to die for what she believed in. "Robert, I have another little surprise for you." Marisa flicked on the power switch to the detonator.

From above, Payton could see the red light go on. "Don't do it, Marisa!"

Mia put the end of her knife to Payton's ribs. Payton knew she would not stab him but how was Marisa to know. Marisa nodded to Payton and he nodded back.

Marisa got a firm grip on the detonator. "Remember the camera you set up in the den? I have the flashcard that shows you going back over in your chair from being shot but what it doesn't show is the blood.

There was no blood on the walls or the floor, not even after the paramedics removed you from the den."

"What does that have to do with anything?"

"I'm sorry, did I say I have the flash-drive? I meant to say, the *L.A. Times* is going to receive it in the mail tomorrow via FedEx."

This new turn of events was enough to have Robert relax his grip just enough for Marisa shift her and Robert's weight to one side which enabled her to turn Robert's back toward the parking lot where the van was parked about 100 feet away. Marisa had one more bit of information. "Robert, one more thing."

"Yeah?"

"Fuck you." With Robert on her back as a shield, Marisa hit the detonator switch and a second after the green light went on, the van exploded.

The shock wave from the explosion blew the doors off the van and ripped open the cargo hold. Tires flew in every direction like balls of flame launched from a catapult. The mushroom fire ball lit up the sky and the boom of the shock wave reached the warehouse. Marisa and Robert were pushed to the ground from the explosion and Robert landed on top of Marisa with all his weight knocking the wind out of her. A piece of burning rubber from one of the tires had hit Robert and the searing rubber lit his clothes on fire. Robert quickly rolled off of Marisa and onto the ground to try to put out the flames. As Robert rolled off, Marisa was able to get her breath back and crawl away from Robert. The flames finally went out as Robert's body became still but continued to smoke.

On the upper floor, Payton and Mia were blown back practically in each other's arms. Payton pushed Mia away from him to find Mia's knife stuck in his thigh.

Mia shook the cob webs off from the explosion, reached for her gun and started to crawl toward Payton. Payton began to back pedal and he crawled over to the edge of the floor to try to find Marisa down below. Payton grabbed an edge of the support beam for leverage to stand, "Marisa!"

Mia pistol whipped Payton into a daze but not unconscious. He fell to his knees and could see Marisa had made it to her feet and was making her way toward the stairwell next to the elevator. Once she got there, the outer wall had caught fire and had begun to burn through.

The smoke from the burning tires had added to the thickness of the air and it was getting hard to breath.

Marisa was near the stairs trying to shield herself from the flames, finding it hard to see from the smoke that was irritating her eyes and drying out her throat.

"Payton!"

Flames began to whip through the dry walls of the old building, making the stairs too much of a risk. Marisa made her way into the elevator and lowered the gate. She hit the third floor button and the elevator lurched and started upward.

Marisa looked up in anticipation of the third floor and saw the two florescent light tubes in the ceiling of the elevator. Marisa reached up and removed one of the lights that caused them both to go out. She taped the end of it on the floor hoping to knock off the end to form a make-shift weapon but all she did was to shatter the entire tube. She quickly reached up and grabbed the other four foot tube but this time lightly taped it against the hand rail that went around the inside of the elevator and it worked. About a third of the tube shattered off and left her with a couple of feet of glass tubing.

The elevator came to a stop. Marisa kept the gate down and stayed inside. A figure was walking toward her through the whirling smoke. It was Mia. Marisa kept her back to the wall of the elevator with the glass sword down at her side, out of sight.

Mia couldn't help but gloat. "My, oh, my. Look what we have here. I see what he sees in you...me."

Marisa really didn't see the similarities, she was used to noticing the details and in her mind. They weren't even close. Marisa couldn't see if Payton was moving from where she was. "Is Payton dead?"

"No, but he soon will be."

Mia tucked her gun into the small of her back, "So it looks like you two were destined to be together, so it shall be. The two lovers found fused together from the intense heat. How does that sound?"

When Mia reached the gate, she lifted the elevator's gate up with both arms. This raised the bullet proof vest she was wearing up enough to expose her lower mid-section. With her left hand still holding up the gate, she reached back with her right and drew her Beretta.

"Kate!" Payton yelled.

When Mia heard Payton call her given name with such force, someplace within her caught her attention and she hesitated for just a moment, and when she did, Marisa lunged forward and stabbed Mia in the abdomen with the florescent tube. She was still holding on to the end of the clear white florescent tube when it began to fill with blood in her hand like a syringe. She felt the surface of the glass get warmer as Mia's blood began to fill the end she was holding. Marisa immediately let go of the tube but Mia gripped onto the gate in immense pain. When the shock had begun to wear off and Mia began to stumble backwards. Her legs faltered as if each step could be her last. Mia only made it a few steps before she collapsed to the floor.

Marisa rushed out of the elevator as the flames were starting to buckle the floor beneath her feet. On her way over to Payton, she walked up to Mia's body and rolled Mia onto her side and removed the Beretta from the small of Mia's back, tucking it in her waist band then continued on over toward Payton. She heard the floor of the elevator crackling and she looked back just as the floor buckled and fell through and the rest of the elevator's shaft went up in flames. When she reached

Payton he was propped up, sitting with his back to one of the support posts. "Are you all right? We have to get out of here."

"What happened to Kate?"

Marisa looked back in her direction and Payton looked over Marisa's shoulder and saw Kate's body lying on the floor with the end of the glass florescent tube sticking out of her. "Look who's saving who, now." Payton tried to stand but it just wasn't happening. "You're going to have to help me pull the knife out of my leg."

"No way!"

"I can guide it, but you're going to have to pull it out."

Payton grabbed the handle of the knife. Marisa placed her hands over his and began to pull upward and out of his leg. Payton screamed, "Ahhhh!"

Payton had Marisa pull her shirt out from her waistband and Payton used the knife to cut a slice about half way up the shirt. Marisa ripped the rest of the lower half of her shirt off and she tied it around Payton's thigh to try to stop the bleeding. She looked at Payton to see if she was hurting him but he wasn't looking at her. He was looking over her shoulder. Marisa turned and looked over her right shoulder and saw Robert standing there next to Mia's body. His face was partially burned from the explosion. His clothes were still smoking a bit and blood was dripping off the end of the barrel of his gun as it hung down next to his side, "Now there's a sight you don't see every day." Marisa's body grew cold with fear at the sound of his voice. "Would you look at that, my wife helping the man who was hired to kill me."

Marisa stood to face Robert.

"Damn you," Marisa cursed.

"I'm afraid you're a little late for that call. I'm just here to take you with me.

Robert tried to raise the gun in his right hand but he was in so much pain he could hardly move it and when he did, it was as if he was in slow motion.

Marisa's eyes grew large and she turned and looked back at Payton. He looked in her eyes then at the Beretta in her waistband. Payton did his best and threw the knife at Robert. As the knife whirled past Robert's head, he ducked to the side a bit and followed the flight of the knife as it flew on past him hitting the wall and caromed back near his feet. Robert began to laugh but it hurt too much so his laughter turned to anger. As he regained his composure, he turned and went to level his gun on Payton, but instead he saw Marisa pointing her Beretta at him. Robert called her bluff. "And what do you think you are you going to with that?"

That was Robert's last thought. Marisa had pulled the trigger and before Robert could register hearing the bang of the gun, the bullet entered the middle of his forehead. He was dead, instantly.

# Chapter 25

"Time to go." Payton's words couldn't have rang more true. The old wooden warehouse had been lit up by the van's explosion. The entrance wall was burning like a roman candle and the flames had reached the pitched roof and had already made their way across. Plus when Mia had previously poured the gas along the back wall Payton knew it was only a matter of a New York minute before the entire building would be an inferno and they were stuck right in the middle of it.

Marisa helped Payton to get to his feet, as he did, he saw Marisa for who she was, not what her husband had made her out to be. "Can you make it?"

"Can you get us out of here?"

Payton walked Marisa over to the open wall. The block and tackle rig was hanging just out of reach, about six feet from them.

"See those chains? You're going to have to jump out, grab onto them, then climb down. Think you can do that?"

Marisa looked at the distance and then at Payton's leg. "I think I can. How about you?"

Payton stepped back a few feet as Marisa took a second look then took a few steps back so she could get a running start.

Payton encouraged her. "The chains are going to swing when you grab onto them so when you grab 'em, hold on. You're going to need to grab two sets at once so you don't automatically start dropping. I know you can do it."

Marisa took her short run, leapt straight out from the edge and grabbed onto the chains. Payton rushed back to the edge to see Marisa clinging to the chains. She had managed to grab just right but her grip was already beginning to slip.

"Remember, use at least two sets of chains to climb down or you could find yourself at the bottom real quick."

Marisa made her way down to the turn buckle then drop to the floor.

Payton saw the entrance in flames and yelled down, "Get in the truck and back out of here, now. I'll be right behind you!"

Marisa ran the cab of the truck as Payton backed up to make his leap. Just as Payton was about to jump, he heard the horn of the truck as Marisa was desperate to get Payton's attention. It worked and he walked back over to the edge as saw Marisa rolling down the passenger side window and yelled to him, "The keys are missing!"

He gave her the okay. "Hold on!"

Payton hobbled over to Mia's body and checked her pockets. No keys. He then checked Robert's and sure enough, Robert had grabbed them for himself. Debris started to fall from the roof and the front side wall. The smoke was getting thick and it was getting harder to breath by the minute and the minutes were quickly running out.

From below Marisa, watched as the back wall lit up and lit up in a hurry, "Payton!"

Payton appeared at the edge of the floor and showed her the keys and tossed them down to her.

Marisa started up the 26 foot truck, put it in reverse and backed it out the main entrance just as one of the doors burned off its hinges, falling and leaving a trail of burning debris blocking the entrance.

Payton waited for the chains to stop swaying. He tucked the gun in his belt, gauged the distance to the chains, and leapt out. He immediately began to go down and fast. He hugged all the chains as best he could to slow his momentum. He caught himself with his feet on the turnbuckle. Suddenly, without warning the rig and Payton dropped to the floor. Where the rig was attached to the warehouse ceiling had burned through and Payton's weight was too much and it all came down, him included.

There was a chain reaction of roof debris that fell onto the upper floor. A few pieces fell onto Mia and bounced off. Mia's body turned and as she rolled onto her back. Mia opened her eyes. She tried to move but the glass tube was still in her abdomen. It had held her from bleeding out. She knew if she took it out she could die but what choice did she have? Mia was able to grab one of the burning pieces of wood that had fallen next to her. She set it next to her body as to have it ready for what she had in mind. Mia grabbed as much of the material of her shirt as she could to stuff into the wound when she pulled out the tube. With her left hand on the tube and her shirt in her right, she pulled the tube out. "Ahhhhh!"

Payton heard Mia's scream as more burning timber was falling all around them.

Mia now had her left hand holding the shirt to her wound as she reached for the smoldering piece of timber. She waved it in the air as best she could to douse and flame then pressed it to her wound right over the material of her shirt cauterizing the shirt into the wound to stop the bleeding. "Ahhhhh!"

More burning debris falling all around. The sound of the crackling wood as it burned was a nightmare and so hot. There was a small window at the entrance for Payton to see the van charging back in through the flames and coming to a stop right next to him.

Payton climbed into the cab through the passenger side. The building was completely engulfed in a raging inferno. Burning debris fell everywhere. The front entrance wall collapsed behind the truck, blocking them in. Some of the roof's debris fell on top of the truck and front end over the engine. The back wall of the warehouse is one complete wall of flame.

Payton saw their only opportunity. "That's our way out."

Marisa looked at the burning wall. More debris fell on the top of the truck with a loud thud as if one of the roof's beams had come down on it, and then another, scaring Marisa and causing her to flinch then double over in pain. "Oh, God, I think I'm bleeding."

Payton reached over and put the van in park then pulled Marisa over his lap to trade places with her. He helped her to get strapped in to her seat belt as more burning timbers fell. Not to waste any more time, he put it in gear and punched the gas pedal. "Hang on."

The truck came crashing through the wall and sent shards of burning debris in all directions.

Inside the cab, Marisa opened her eyes after the impact with the wall to see some of the burning debris was still on the hood of the truck. "The truck is on fire!"

Payton hit the brakes in hopes to get the debris to slide off. As the truck skid to a halt in the open field behind the warehouse, the debris on the hood slid off onto the ground. What they weren't ready for was the debris from the top of the truck to land on the hood of the engine as it slid forward. And part of the debris was Mia. She had the knife in her hand, her clothes were smoldering and her hair was partially singed from the blaze. Marisa screamed at the sight of Mia. "Ahhhhh!"

Payton quickly reached down and grabbed the Beretta from his belt and fired three rounds through the windshield. The windshield shattered into multiple spider webbed patterns from the rounds as they passed through and hit Mia in the chest. The three consecutive center mass impacts sent Mia flying backwards off the hood. Mia's body spun as it fell to the ground, and on impact, rolled a few times and stopped face down.

Marisa was curled up on the seat with her hands over her ears from the loud pops from the gun going off in the confined space of the cab. She held her head and turned away her face to not see what happened.

Payton put his hand on her shoulder. "Marisa, are you alright? Marisa?

Marisa unfolded herself and looked at Payton. Payton slid over across the bench seat next to her, reached across her body, undid her belt, and took her in his arms.

Marisa had her head down against Payton's chest. She could hear his heartbeat so clearly and yet wondered, "How can a man stay so calm? Could such a man have feelings and truly be able to share them the way she dreamed of?" What was it going to take for her to know for sure? "Payton?" She felt his heartbeat louder at the sound of her voice. "Is it over? Is this the end?"

Payton knew it would never be over as long as Delgado was alive. His thoughts of having to leave Marisa in order to save her felt like a curse. Marisa felt Payton's breathing get deeper and his heart to beat faster, giving her hope.

Payton brushed his hand through her hair. "It's not over."

Marisa felt her heart sink. She looked up and saw in his eyes that what he felt was true. He knew he had to go away and make things right before they could ever have a chance together. "I'm going to have to go away soon and I don't know when I will be back."

As much as Marisa wanted to beg Payton to stay, she knew he had to go but for how long she didn't know. "When?"

"Soon."

"Why?"

"When Delgado finds out you killed his nephew, he won't stop until you are dead. So I'm going to have to find a way to get to him first."

"What am I supposed to do in the meantime, hide?"

"No. I want you to go on with your life..."

"What life?"

"I want you to take this money and live the life you always wanted. Travel, find your passion and run with it."

"You make it sound like it so easy just to start over."

"It is...take this chance you have been giving and live the life you want."

"If it's that easy, then do it with me. Start over."

There was a long pause and her words came from her heart. She had never spoken so freely before.

Payton knew what she was asking but it would all have to wait. "Marisa, there's got to be more than ten million dollars in the back of this truck. Find someone you can trust and slowly invest the cash in real estate and sell it short but not too short, it might send up a red flag. After a few deals you will have clean money and you can open the studio you've always wanted."

"I can't take the money, but you can. No one knows who you are, you can use it to do what you have to do then start again."

"I still have too much of a past that I have to account for."

"Where are you going to go?"

"To try to make things safer for you."

"Well, where ever you end up in your travels, will you at least send me a postcard so I know you are still alive?"

Marisa felt a deep cramping in her gut and flexed hard.

"Let's not worry about that now, you need a doctor."

Payton slid back behind the wheel, pulling Marisa up next to him. He put the truck in gear and pulled further away from the fiery grave of one Roberto Delgado. Payton took a look back to see if and when the last of the warehouse would fall and thought he saw a car drive around from the side of the building. His only thought was, whoever was coming to check out the fire, he hoped they didn't get a good look at the plates on the moving truck as they pulled away.

The car stopped not too far from where Mia's body was lying on the ground. The driver got out and saw the back of the moving truck as it made its way down the back road and off into the distance. Tony had a good idea who it was. He had decided no matter how much money he had with him in the tires Marisa had given him, it wasn't enough to stop General Delgado from sending his men after him, so he returned to the warehouse where he was originally headed when Payton and Marisa had hijacked him and switch out vehicles with him.

Tony was caught off guard when he heard the compressor tank explode inside the warehouse. He ducked instinctively and knelt down near Mia's body. He had to know. He cautiously rolled her over and checked her pulse. It was low, but she had one.

# Chapter 26

The moving van was parked on the street under the canopy of light from the street lamp making it less likely to be tampered with at such a late hour. It was the closest one nearest the entrance of the Desert Springs Hospital Medical Center on Flamingo Drive, which was in the middle of Las Vegas just east off of Highway 15 and north of the McCarran Airport.

An ambulance pulled up to the emergency entrance and the EMT's removed a patient, wheeling the patient into the hospital just as Payton came out. Marisa was in surgery and there was nothing he could do except stay out of the way. The less he was seen the better. He watched a plane fly over as it was making its turn taking passengers to places unknown. Something Payton thought sounded pretty good right about now. He climbed into the moving van and headed toward the main strip.

Before he got too close, he stopped in a quiet place along the road next to a trash can and removed a few empty plastic bags from a bin. He opened the back of the van and nonchalantly took out bundles of cash equaling what he thought would be about $30,000.

As he drove up to the gas station, he noticed a parking spot open off to the side and took it. Payton locked up the van figuring if anyone noticed they would just think it might be an empty rental. He grabbed his two bags of cash and headed off to the Hard Rock Hotel and Casino. Payton had been there before and knew the layout. He wanted someplace familiar as not to waste any more time than necessary. His goal was to get to as many tables as it took to buy in a few thousand at a time, play as few hands as possible and get out, hopefully even, and without drawing too much attention.

$$\neq$$

The doctor took a final look at Marisa's chart and left Marisa to the nurse who was on duty. "Just let her rest. I'll be back to check on her soon."

Payton was waiting in the hall by Marisa's room. Payton greeted the doctor as he came out of her room, "How is she? Can I see her?"

"Are you family?"

"Yes, I'm her brother. I'm the one who filled out her admission forms."

"Did you know about her condition?"

"We had been talking about the possibility of her being pregnant and her wanting to start a family while trying to launch a new career at the same time just the other day."

"Can you tell me what happened that caused her to lose the child? She looked like she has been through a lot recently."

"We were doing some remodeling on her new studio and had just finished when we had a small fire in a trash barrel in the back trash bin. She tried to put it out on her own. Luckily I was there and we got it out but she must have put a lot of strain on herself. A little while later she complained of some cramping and then when we found out there was some bleeding, I rushed her over here.

"Where is the father?"

"They were recently separated."

"Then it's a good thing you were there for her."

"Yes, I suppose it was. How is she?"

"Marisa's going to be fine but the trauma she suffered was just too much. We've done what we can to make her comfortable for now and I don't see any reason why she shouldn't be able to go home tomorrow."

"Can I talk to her now?"

"Yes, that would be fine. Just keep it brief. She's going to need plenty of rest."

"Thank you."

Marisa was lying in the dimly lit room. Her eyes were closed as Payton entered. He walked up next to her bed and took her hand. She slowly opened her eyes.

Payton's first thought was it was all his fault but in the end came to terms with if he wasn't there, she would be dead. "The doctor says you're going to be okay."

Marisa could barely keep her eyes to open to see that it was Payton before she closed them once more. "Payton?"

"Yes, I'm here."

Payton gripped her hand a bit tighter and gently rubbed his thumb over the back of her hand.

Marisa mouth was dry from the anesthesia. "Why?"

Marisa tried to reach up and brush her hair away from her face but was still groggy so Payton tenderly brushed her hair back for her and adjusted her pillows so she could sit up. "I was worried." Marisa smiled as Payton continued to pay attention to her. "The doctor said there's a good chance you can go home as soon as tomorrow."

"And what about you? Where is home for you?"

Payton pulled up a chair next to the bed and took a seat, knowing he wasn't going anywhere until he knew for sure she was going to be alright. "I have no real family. My brother and I were raised by our grandparents after our folks took off on a trip and never came back. Later we had heard our dad was in jail and our mom ran off with another man. When we got old enough, my brother and I joined the Army, and he was killed on his first tour. After that, my job became everything to me."

"So you became a sniper and that is where you met Kate?"

Payton could see Marisa was fading in and out, so he figured it was safe to talk about it since she probably wouldn't remember anyway. "Yes. We were assigned as a team right away. She was a great spotter and we developed a short hand pretty fast and made a good team."

"So what happened? What caused you to become an assassin? The money?"

"It was never the money. Our position was being over ran and we knew we would never make it back to our rendezvous in time, so we burned everything we could before they captured us. We knew a rescue was out of the question once they had us in their tunnels. Kate's final option was to die or go someplace in her mind where she was no longer Kate."

"So she became Mia."

"Yes."

As out of it as Marisa was, she could tell Mia had meant much more to him than just being his spotter. She closed her eyes to try to imagine what such a change in one's life would do to someone but didn't have to go far from her own, "Now that, that part of your life is over, what are you going to do?" Marisa was looking for some sort of sign from Payton that he was willing to try to stick around and share his life with her.

"It's not over."

Marisa opened her eyes so she could read his sincerity.

Payton continued, "There are too many loose ends and they will come after me to get to you so, it's not over. The only way to be sure is I'm going to have to go after them—the men that I have done work for in the past that are helping Delgado get into power."

"How many more lives do you have to take before you can live your own?"

Payton didn't answer her question but he did hint he wanted to be free to be himself and in Marisa's mind that meant, free to come back to her. "I'm not sure how long it will take, but when I am done, you will be able to live your life without having to look over your shoulder, and I will be obligated to no one."

Payton could see the weight of the whole day in Marisa's eyes as she had to close them once again since the drugs were still taunting her to rest but she tried as best she could to hold on, to keep talking to Payton, hoping if she could keep him there longer, it would be harder for him to leave.

The doctor walked in and Payton took the opportunity to walk out. Marisa opened her eyes to saw her doctor standing over her. "Your brother didn't want you to have to worry. He has taken care of all of your hospital expenses."

"My brother?"

"Yes, Payton. He insisted on waiting until you were out of the woods, but I told him, I thought you were going to be just fine and more than likely would be able to go home tomorrow." Dr. Yoshino took Marisa's hand in his. "I have to ask you, Marisa, where you aware you were pregnant?"

"I suspected. But with what has happened..."

"Yes, Payton mentioned you were under a lot of stress and recently had a fire at your studio."

Marisa went along with what the doctor was saying but had already concluded from the word *were* she had lost the baby. She knew it was all for the best but instead of feeling just relieved, she also felt the pain for the loss for a child she had always wanted, which only made her think of wanting one with a man like Payton even more. Marisa's mind was in a fog for the few minutes the doctor was talking to her about the trauma she had suffered as the cause for the miscarriage, which may have done enough damage to prevent her from having children in the future. By the time her doctor had finished his explanation, she had already let go of the dream of one day starting a family.

As the Doctor slid the chair back into the corner, Marisa noticed Payton's jacket still lying there across the arm. "Where did Payton go?"

"Looks like his keys are here so I'm am sure he hasn't gone too far. I can see you two are very close. You're very lucky to have had family around to help you when you did."

Marisa only caught the last bit of what the doctor was saying. "What's that?"

"You and Payton, it's nice to see the love you two have for each other and if things were different, you would be there for him."

Marisa felt the deep sentiment of his words, "Yes."

# Chapter 27

ONE YEAR LATER

It was Election Day in Mexico City and General Delgado was on the platform about to claim his victory of El Salvador's Presidential race even before it was official. Delgado knew his place in history was bought and paid for many times over by a few of the right men in the right places at the right time and for Delgado this was his day. He walked up to the podium and began to wave to the crowd as the press continued to click away one photo after another. Delgado was not affected by the crowds distaste for him as boos seem to outweigh the cheers for him and his entourage.

Delgado made his way to the edge of the platform, leaned over, and shook a few hands to satisfy the photographers. He continued to wave and play the part of the man with the answers to his country's problems.

Cameras followed his every move. One journalist turned and stepped into view of one of the cameras making sure to leave a shot line over his shoulder of Delgado. "With the election being held today, can this former guerrilla commando who has unconfirmed ties to a local drug cartel, truly do be a man of his word and bring back the hope to his country for a better tomorrow? Can this self-proclaimed leader stand up and be accountable or is he merely filling the shoes of his handlers?"

Delgado paused once again for a photo opportunity. The camera followed him with a tight head and shoulder shot, then stopped as Delgado stood proud and erect in the center of the shot.

There was a click. The camera that was currently following Delgado, was not a camera, but a high powered rifle scope. The "click" was the rifle's cross hairs being rotated into view.

Payton had just checked the flags on stage as they were hanging still on this hot dry day, which made for ideal conditions for such a shot from this distance. Payton took a deep breath, then let it out slowly, then closed his eyes for a moment. When he opened his eyes again, Delgado was still lined up in the cross hairs of the rifle. Payton could feel his breathing slow and found that place in between heartbeats that every sniper called home and was at peace with what he was doing was for the greater good.

Payton was in the zone and squeezed the trigger. Click. The rifle he had acquired down here for this job had jammed. Payton cleared the round and as it flipped from the rifle's port, it slipped into the protective overalls Payton was wearing over his other set of clothes. Payton wasn't one to panic. He went through his routine and had Delgado once again in his sights and BANG! From over 1000 yards away, just over a half a mile, Delgado dropped dead.

The crowd began running in all directions as Delgado's body hit the ground almost immediately upon impact of the bullet hitting him between the eyes. One of the female celebrities that was on hand for the press coverage was standing just behind Delgado and to the side in her white designer dress. A dress that was now splashed on one side with Delgado's blood and a piece of his skull cap was lodged into her bare shoulder like a piece of shrapnel. Her screams of shock and terror could be heard over the cries of the crowd's roar of panic.

One of Delgado's security detail looked through a pair of high powered binoculars in the direction of where he thought the direction of the shot came from and saw a man with long blonde hair with workman's overalls standing near an open window and pointed, "There, up there!" It was a woman's voice. In all of the commotion, the woman got bumped and when she did, she lost her hat and the scarf that was hiding her face. As the scarf came loose, it exposed some minor scaring that ran down one side of her face and along her neck. The burns had healed but you could still see the woman that was once Kate now bearing the scars of Mia. She keyed the walkie-talkie, "The Fiesta Grand Hotel!"

A patrol car pulled up to the front of the hotel from where Payton had taken his shot. Two security men exited the patrol car, drew their pistols, and ran into the lobby of the Hotel.

There were two sets of elevators. Both were on the way down. The two security men trained the weapons on the doors of the elevators. Ding. The doors opened on one of the elevators and a few guests began to file out and were startled from the guns pointed in their direction. No Payton. Ding. The other door opened to the second elevator. Again the guest and staff exiting the elevator were taken back by the guns pointed at them. No Payton. One of the security men entered one of the elevators and hit the button to the top floor as the other man waited in the lobby. The doors closed. As the crowd walked off the elevator and passed the remaining security man, he noticed a well-dressed American businessman with dark short hair in a tux.

A woman in the lobby began to cough and need some water. As she went to take a drink, someone in the crowd bumped her, and she spilled some water on Payton. Payton pulled his handkerchief from his jacket pocket, and in doing so, pulled out the jammed round. The round that had slipped into his overalls had made its way into Payton's suit pocket unbeknownst to him and as he pulled out the handkerchief, it fell out and hit the floor. Its brass casing landed with a clang.

The security guard turned and saw the loose round spinning on the floor at Payton's feet. Payton was faster and had the security man in a headlock and in seconds had him passing out from the choke hold but not before he had got off a shot off in the struggle.

Payton had been grazed on the outside of his left bicep. He stuffed his handkerchief in his jacket sleeve from the inside to help stop the bleeding. He quickly made his way out of the lobby with the rest of the crowd to the streets.

The security man who took the first elevator was checking door handles of rooms with windows that faced the town square. The third room he was about to check, the door was already slightly open, and he cautiously entered.

All he found was Payton's rifle, a blond wig with a set of overalls, and a single bullet that was left sitting on the window sill.

Payton had made his way down the street with the rest of the crowd. He stopped next to a street-side mailbox. He removed a postcard addressed to Marisa from the inside pocket of his jacket. On the back all he had written was, "Coming home." Just as he dropped the postcard into the mailbox, he noticed his thumb print in blood on the corner of the postcard. It was too late to do anything about it, the postcard was on its way.

# Chapter 28

Marisa had parked halfway between the deli and her studio's loft. She stepped into the deli and ordered her usual crispy chicken salad to go. While she was waiting she had noticed one of the newspapers that had been left on one of the tables. She took a glance at the week old headlines. "El Salvador. President Elect. Assassinated."

The man behind the counter called Marisa's name and took her out of the trance she was in as she was momentarily taken back to a year ago when Payton was telling her about his time there.

Marisa made her way down to her studio and was let in by her assistant, Sara. As the door closed, in bold lettering, the sign read: Payton, Ink. The studio Marisa had always envisioned was up and running and doing well but wouldn't have even got off the ground if it wasn't for Payton so she thought it only appropriate to name it after him. The main lobby was filled with beautiful images that Marisa had taken herself of men and woman in erotic poses and provocative new artistic choices making her website one the hottest trending sites.

Marisa sat down to eat her lunch. Sara came in and placed the day's mail in the corner basket which sat on the edge of her desk. Sara was excited to be working with one of the world's top models who just happened to be in town for the day. This model was a fan of Marisa's website and wanted to come by and say, "Hello."

Sara was in frenzy. "Patrizia just called and will be here in a few minutes."

"That's great. Is studio 'A' ready?"

"Yes. Both cameras have new batteries and fresh flashcards in them."

"Great. Let me know when you see her car pull up. I'd like to be in the studio ready to go."

Sara took her cue and when out to the reception area, sat at her desk below the sign on the wall that read "AMOROUS" and waited anxiously. Marisa finished her salad and reached for the mail. She began to thumb through it when she got the word Patrizia had arrived. She flopped the mail back into the in-box and out slid about one-third of Payton's postcard from Mexico City from the middle of the pile.

Studio "A" was the larger of the two rooms set up for almost any type of photography. The back was painted green and at the bottom rolled smoothly to the floor. Marisa's equipment was state of the art and her cameras were set up with wireless feeds to the computers and the large monitor that was off to one side for instant feedback. The lights were on and the room was hot and ready to go.

"Marisa!" Patrizia had let out an enthusiastic hello to her new found friend. The beautiful 5'10" blonde Italian model out-stretched her arms and was already hugging Marisa before she could get out two words.

"Hello, Patrizia. How are you? It's finally nice to meet you."

Patrizia Villa, who had dropped her last name as most models do when they reach a certain status in their careers, spoke perfect English, French, as well as her native Italian. "I am just fine. Thank you for having me. Your place looks wonderful."

"Thank you. We have a great time here and we like to keep it light."

"And I especially love the title of your on-line magazine, *Amorous*. It says it all. It's erotic, it's about passion, and it's sexy as hell. I love it."

"Thanks. It took a while then we finally settled on *Amorous*."

"I love what you did on the San Francisco shoot for last month's cover."

"We did it all right here."

"No way."

"Would you like me to show you how we did it?"

"Sure, let's have some fun, shall we."

Marisa turned to Sara, "Can to go next door to studio 'B' and see if Jesse is done shooting over there and if he can stop by and say hello to Patrizia?"

Sara left the two new best friends alone long enough to go next door as Marisa began to show Patrizia the lay-out of the studio. A moment later Sara returned with Jesse.

Jesse was a 6 foot specimen of a 30 year old hunk and when he saw Patrizia, his grin gave away everything, including that million dollar smile. Jesse held out his hand, "Hello, Patrizia, nice to meet you."

Patrizia skipped the hand shake and just put her hands on Jesse's chest and gave a little cat claw move over his pecs. "Hello." Patrizia turned and looked at Marisa. "Let's play."

Marisa pulled up a green box about the size of a podium and had Patrizia lean onto it using her elbows and positioned Jesse behind her a bit. Marisa got her camera ready. "Jesse, can you remove your shirt?"

Both Sara and Patrizia chimed in together, "Yes, Jesse..." and all the girls had a collective laugh as Jesse unbuttoned his shirt and pulled it off. Marisa continued, "Now roll it up as if you at going to snap it and flick Patrizia across the ass."

Patrizia played along. "Yes, please, Jesse."

Jesse whipped the shirt into a tight rope as Patrizia leaned forward onto the box just lifting her toes off the ground and slightly bending one leg. Her long legs went up and they made quite an ass out of themselves and Marisa began to shutter off a dozen images in a matter of seconds when Jesse made his playful snap.

Marisa called out, "Thanks, that should do it."

"What, that's it?" Patrizia was just getting warmed up.

"That's it. Look here." Marisa pulled up the images that were automatically downloaded to the computer. She quickly found the best one and loaded the graphics of last week's cover from the San Francisco shot of a girl leaning off a rail at Pier 39. But now it was Patrizia in her place and Jesse snapping his shirt on her backside.

"Wow. That is great." Patrizia impressed.

Marisa hit a button and out came an 8 X 10 of the shot fresh off the printer and she handed it to Patrizia. "All yours."

"Thank you, darling. This was so much fun I will have to definitely come back and spend the whole day with you and we can go shopping and do all those things best friends do."

The silent doorbell light flashed in the studio and Sara went to answer the front door. A moment later she arrived with a box of a dozen red roses.

Patrizia made a fun little joke with Jesse as she wrapped her arms around his broad shoulders, "Oh, Jesse, You didn't have to…"

Sara quickly crushed her hopes. "He didn't. These are for Marisa."

Patrizia interest was piqued. "From who?"

"It doesn't say from whom. It just says, 'Happy 1st Anniversary.'"

"Ah, Marisa must have a secret admirer," Patrizia said with a smile.

"Secret, yes." Sara chimed in, "Admirer, maybe."

"That's enough, ladies," Marisa tries to play it off but her excitement is hard to hide. She took the dozen long stem roses into her office and laid them on the desk. That's when she noticed the postcard that was sticking out the pile of mail. She slipped it out and saw the picture on the cover of the Palacio de Bellas Artes, the Fine Arts Palace, which was located in Mexico City that was completed in 1934.

She turned it over and immediately recognized the hand writing that read: "Coming home" as Payton's. But what she hoped was not his, was the thumb print in dried blood.

# Chapter 29

Payton's thumb print was all Marisa could think about as she sat behind her office desk at home. She had redecorated the office that her husband Robert had once used for himself, but after the remodel, she felt she had made it her own. The office was now decorated nicely with complimentary colors of summer. Blues to capture the sky and water and a warm inviting sunset orange to reflect her favorite time of the day. On the walls were pictures she and Payton had taken. A couple of the pictures were of her from when Payton had taken her photo when he was on the beach observing her from a distance. Others were some of her early work at Payton, Ink. and cover art from her first days of the on-line magazine, AMOROUS, going active. Marisa spun her chair around and pulled a small journal from her shelf and laid it on the desk. She opened it and flipped through the first few pages then came to a postcard from Paris. She couldn't help but dream about what it would have been like if she had actually been there with Payton.

*Payton and Marisa were walking hand in hand along the River Seine that flowed through Paris and alongside the Eiffel Tower. The day couldn't have been any better. The sun was out and the sounds and smells of spring were in the air. For Marisa it was her first time in Paris but she knew Payton had been here before as she remembered waking up that morning at his place in his souvenir t-shirt from the original city of lights. As they approached one of the local street venders, Payton offered to buy Marisa a Falafel but she had to turn it down as she was still full from the crepes Payton had made for her that morning.*

*One of the tour boats was passing by on the Seine and Marisa went over to the water's edge to take in all that was Paris. Payton had his digital 35mm camera hanging around his neck. He brought it up to his eye and began taking pictures of Marisa as only he could, with all that he felt for her framing each shot. Marisa took a look back and saw Payton with the camera and began doing some fun poses as well as the serious ones for posterity. When it was all over she laughed, ran back up into Payton's arms and kissed the man she adored with every* bit of passion she could give to let him know, she was his and he was hers, from now on.

Marisa flipped to the next page of her journal and saw the postcard from Puerta del Sol which was located in the center of Madrid, Spain. How she longed to have been there with Payton as well. She had read up on it and learned it meant "Gate of the Sun." She saw herself and Payton spending New Year's with the many of thousands who did each year.

*They took their time as they strolled and admired the architecture that surrounded them. It was almost midnight and they were standing below the clock waiting to hear it chime in the New Year just outside the Casa de Correos headquarters. Marisa was showing Payton the pictures she had taken earlier of him under the famous Strawberry Tree that stood on one side of Puerta de Sol and was considered a symbol of Madrid.*
    *The crowd began to count down to the New Year in many different languages and the excitement of all these people coming together for this moment was something Marisa would never want to forget.*

The grandfather clock in Marisa's office struck one. Her heart was filled with what could have been, if only these postcards were actual pictures she herself had taken. She flipped the next page in the journal and saw the previous postcard she had received from Payton about three months ago from Venice, Italy.

*Marisa looked across the table at Payton, picked up the camera, and took a few pictures of him just looking at her. She wanted to try to capture that look he gave her when she caught him looking at her in bed. "It's all in the eyes," she thought. She panned around and took a few pictures of the locals as well as the tourists who were milling around St. Mark's Square. She could see why everyone came here, it was beautiful. She scrolled back through the images from earlier of their visit to St. Mark's Basilica, the Doge's Palace, and the Museo Correr.*

*The Correr Museum was located along the south side of the square on the upper floor of the Procuratorie Nuove. The museum had asked Marisa not to take any pictures inside but the art work was breathtaking and she was able to squeeze off a few without anyone really noticing. A nobleman by the name of Teodoro Correr had left the collection along with funds to keep the place open to the public back in the 1830's. Payton had given her the history of the place but she really wasn't listening as much as she just liked hearing Payton being passionate about art and history.*

*As they finished their drinks outside one of the many cafe's that lined the square, Marisa closed her eyes, took in the ambiance and a deep breath.*

When she opened her eyes, the reality of the situation struck her as she sat behind her desk and turned the next page in the journal, it was blank. Marisa was about to slip the postcard in its protective sleeve when she noticed the date stamp on the back. It was from one week ago. Around the same time as the headlines she saw on the paper down in the deli.

Marisa wiggled the mouse on her desk and her computer screen came up and she went to Google to see if she could find out any more information on the unsolved assassination of the President elect in Mexico City. Then she made the connection, even though the assassination was in Mexico City, it was for the President of El Salvador and that's when she saw the name: Delgado.

Marisa's heart began to race. She knew deep down inside it was Payton. His words came back to her, "There are too many loose ends..."

Marisa flipped back to the front page of the journal to the postcard from Paris. She checked the postmark then entered the date from nine months earlier into the computer and crossed referenced it to unsolved murders in or around the city of Paris, France.

There were a few to choose from but there was just one that said it had ties to Central America. The victim's name was Marcus Lambert. The article went onto to say he was a suspected of using his resources for illegal smuggling of cocaine. He was a named partner in a local museum where it was a suspected he was using his museum as a front to import the drugs from Central America as a way to bring in cocaine into Italy as artifacts. Since the case was ongoing, the article went onto say the police could not elaborate on the investigation.

Marisa's vision of her beautiful day with Payton suddenly turned dark, as dark as night. She had tried to keep the truth about Payton in the past and keep it there but the reality soon poisoned her thoughts and poured into her heart.

*Nine months earlier...*

There was no moon out as Marcus Lambert was out for his nightly stroll through the park. It was a quiet night except for off in the distance you could hear the faint sound of a fog horn. The path he was on was lit by lamp posts that had been around since the turn of the century. Every fifty yards or so was a park bench. As Marcus walked his Shih Tzu, Jude, down the path, he could see the bench that he used to stop for a short break on was occupied by a two men who looked to be homeless. One man was asleep and the other man was in the process of shoving old newspapers in his worn out jacket for insulation to keep warm for the night. As Marcus approached, the man stopped long enough to reach into his pocket and he tossed the Shih Tzu a treat, which the dog immediately gobbled down before Marcus could pull him back.

"Hey, would mind not feeding my dog?"

The homeless just mumbled back a few words that didn't seem to make sense. The man then gathered his belongings, stood up, and walked away. Marcus had noticed the man had left what appeared to be his wallet. Marcus grabbed it and called out to the man, "Hey, fella, you left your wallet."

The man kept on walking and talking to himself so Marcus figured he didn't hear him so he quickly walked up to the man and just before he went to tap him on the should, Payton turned and shoved a home-made shiv into Lambert's gut with three quick consecutive jabs. Lambert went down dead in a heap. Payton grabbed his wallet and went back over to the bench and put the wallet and the shiv in amongst the other man's things and left. As Payton walked away he didn't feel too bad for the homeless man he had drugged with a sandwich he had given him an hour earlier. He figured the guy would at least get three square meals and some good health care. Taking out Lambert was his only concern as Lambert was indeed one of Delgado's associates and had been funding Delgado's take-over of El Salvador.

Marisa turned back another page and revealed the postcard from Madrid. Again she checked the postmark against unsolved murders from the region.

The story that stood out was about a man by the name of Estevon Valdez who was killed in an explosion six months ago, two days after the post mark on the post card. Marisa went onto read about the man's past convictions to gun running but most of the charges had been dropped due to evidence tampering and witness refusing to testify. It was long suspected they were threatened but in the end, no evidence.

*Six months ago…*

Estevon Valdez had been very careful to lock up the safe before letting his men go home for the night. The safe held about one million dollars give or take. Especially take since Estevon had been skimming off the top before sending Delgado his share on the gun sales from which Delgado had been exporting out of El Salvador thru the Panama Canal to the coastal port of Porto Pesqueiro in Vigo, Spain then over land by trucks to Madrid. Vigo was on the west coast of Spain north of Portugal which was a bit out of the way but that is what Delgado wanted.

The 18 wheeler would truck the weapons which took up half the load of which the other half was fresh vegetables, inland. That way when the driver stopped at check points along the way of his bi-monthly route to Madrid, the driver would make his normal exchange of pleasantries, and drop off a bit of the fresh vegetables to his connections and then continue on his way. Before reaching Madrid, the driver would stop in the town of Cuellar which was about half way between Palencia and Madrid. Cuellar had a population of about ten thousand so it was quiet enough to use as distribution hub for the weapons. From there, Delgado didn't care where or to whom they were sold as long as he got his cut on time.

Estevon was greedy and was using some of Delgado's products to make bombs for his clients. It wasn't enough to sell the guns and explosives at a good profit, Estevon had gained quite a reputation as a bomb maker. After selling the C-4 to his clients he would then offer to make the bombs to their specs for another fee. A large fee.

Estevon went into his backroom that was located in the back of his office and to go over the latest specs for one of his clients. The specs called for a cell phone trigger. That way all the client had to do was to call the number that went to the trigger phone from another phone, preferably a burner as not to be traced, and set off the device. Estevan knew all he had to do was connect one last wire for the client and the weapon that was designed to take out a standard size car would be ready.

Estevon jumped when a cell phone rang that was under a towel on his work bench. He found the phone and answered it, "Hello, who is this?"

Payton replied, "This is your client, Mr. Veldez. I just wanted to make sure my order is ready."

Estevon was about to say, "I will have it ready for you shortly," but he then noticed the work on the device had been completed.

Payton was a few blocks away and had watched the rest of Estevon's men leave through the lens of his high powered scope from his sniper rifle and he also knew his target was alone. Payton knew the device was ready as well because he himself had finished it the night before and had switched out the burner phones that would trigger the bomb. It was his specs he had contracted Valdez to create under a false identity. Payton knew Estevon's routine and when would be the best time to put his plan in motion and it had gone off without a hitch, "Mr. Valdez, are you there?"

"Yes..."

Payton took out a second burner phone and hit redial on the pre-programmed number.

The cell phone on the bomb lit up as it started to ring. On the second ring, Alverez reached for his wire cutters and just as he got the cutters up to the wire, the third ring was the last thing Alverez heard.

$\neq$

Marisa turned the third page to the postcard she had received from Payton three months ago on his trip to Venice, Italy. It didn't take long to find another unsolved murder of a corrupt politician who was assassinated one day before the post mark she found on the back of the post card.

*Three months ago…*

Lamar Costa was on his 50 ft. Azimut yacht anchored about 200 yards off the coast of Venice. The island itself was located in the Venetian Lagoon which stretched along the shoreline at the north end of the Adriatic Sea. He had three guards on board who also doubled as staff and made sure he had what he needed to entertain his guest. Today his two guests were two of the eight women that were up for auction and going to the highest bidder, but first he wanted to have his play time with them. He didn't care he could be their father or even if their father's knew where they were.

Costa was below deck in the master stateroom and he had both girls stripped down to their panties. One girl was massaging his feet and the other massaging his scalp and he couldn't wait for them to meet in the middle. The sun was just going down and one guard had been preparing dinner for all six of them in the galley while the other two held watch.

One guard was at the stern, fishing, facing south while the other was above on the Flybridge Helm focusing his attention to the north. The guard fishing noticed he had a bite and took the rod in hand and began to reel in his catch. The glare from the sunset was making it hard to see below the surface but he knew the fish would be breaking the surface any minute now. He only took his eye off the pole for a second to wipe his brow but that was when Payton broke the surface of the water and shot the guard in the chest twice from his silenced Beretta he had wrapped in a baggie.

Payton boarded quickly and took out the second guard above as he must have heard the sound of the other guard hitting the deck. "Piff. Piff." The second guard went down and as he fell, he landed almost standing up as his body landed up against the support post of the canopy of the Flybridge. Payton pulled off the baggie from the gun to get a better grip. His wetsuit had a small utility belt that held two extra clips if needed, but Payton was so focused, nothing was going to get in his way of taking out Costa.

The third guard heard someone behind him and just thought it was one of his fellow guards. He turned with a sauce pan in his hand a spoon in the other as if to ask, "Taste this and tell me what you think?" But his answer was two rounds from Payton's Beretta. As the man went down, Payton reached out and grabbed the sauce pan before it hit the ground and set it back on the burner. Payton was kind enough to turn off the burners as they were no longer going to be used this evening.

Payton entered the stateroom just as one of the girls was about to take away the towel that was pitching a tent over his mid-section. Costa saw the end of the silencer trained between his eyes. Payton motioned to the girls and said, "Get dressed."

Costa recognized Payton and felt betrayed. "Who sent you, Delgado?"

"No, I'm here on my own."

"Then why are you here?"

"Some things are just not for sale."

Costa thought he was talking about the girls but Payton was referring to himself and cleaning up the mess he helped Delgado create. The girls finished getting dressed and Payton asked them to go outside to wait on the back deck of the yacht.

As the two girls passed through the yacht, their screams indicated each time they found another guard dead.

Costa had one last question, "Is there any amount of money I can offer you?"

Payton squeezed off two rounds. "Piff. Piff."

"Nope."

$$\neq$$

Marisa put the postcard with Payton's blood stained thumb print on it into the journal, closed it and asked herself out loud, "Payton, what have you done?"

## Chapter 30

Marisa was relaxing in the late afternoon sun having taken the rest of the day off, spending the time pondering her feelings for Payton. She slipped off her sandals, slid her feet off the edge of the beach towel and dug her feet into the warm sand.

A lot had happened over the last year. The life she thought she had was not truly her own. She had been a centerpiece for her husband, the victim of a car accident that cost her the lives of both her parents, then she came face to face with the man who was hired to kill her and instead fell in love with him. At the time, it was the passion of the moment and how life can make you forget about reality and the consequences it can be over just living in the moment, which after having survived, she chose to just live. No regrets.

That is when she knew she had true feelings for Payton. Was it love? Yes, she thought it was, up until she found the link to the unsolved murders from the postcards Payton had sent. Why did he send them? Was it about full disclosure, wanting her to know what he was doing was clearing his name and taking out the men who were the prime associates of Delgado? It had to be, what else could it be?

Payton had risked his life for her. There had to be something between them that was worth fighting for and that was when Marisa knew she had a love for him that would last forever. She seemed to have everything she ever wanted including her freedom.

Marisa let the sound of the waves crashing onto the beach take over her senses. The wind with its familiar scent of the ocean's crisp air whipping through her hair at will. She could feel the warmth of the sun caressing her shoulders remembering what it was like to be in Payton's arms. His lips kissing her neck as he tasted the passion that was her desire for him.

The postcard said he was coming home soon and that was over a week ago. That filled her heart and soul like nothing else. He gave her strength and a compassion for life she knew she never had and that was why she loved him. She stood up and took off her light weight white cotton blouse.

From a long distance, Marisa was being watched through a set of high powered binoculars. As the lens was re-focused, Marisa could be seen undoing her bikini top and dropping it to the beach towel as she then walked to the edge of the water only wearing her worn-in faded Levi shorts. She tested the water with her toe, then walked into the surf up to her waist and felt the power of the small wave slap against her as she held her ground.

Payton walked over the dune and down towards the water's edge carrying just a small back pack over one shoulder just as Marisa dove head first into the oncoming wave. When she came up, the water was just below her shoulders. She turned to head back to shore before the next wave but was pleasantly surprised to see Payton standing by her towel. She slowly walked from the water not wanting to blink just in case it was a dream. The first wave pushed her forward and lashed her wet hair around, causing it to cling her neck and shoulders. The next wave washed against the back of her long silky legs and it was as if it was Payton's hands had caressed her.

As Marisa got closer, Payton reached down and grabbed her towel to wrap around her shoulders and cover her bare breasts that were glistening from the sunlight refracting off the rain of sea water that traveled down over them from any of the viewing public down the beach. Marisa didn't even notice them, she was not looking away from Payton's eyes as he was looking at her like no other man had.

Payton went to wrap her up and she pushed away the towel and instead, wrapped her arms around Payton's neck, and pressed her wet body up as close as she could to his. Payton could feel her wet breasts firmly against him and his hands folded around her body. The two shared a romantic kiss as if they were the only two on the beach.

"Welcome home, Payton."

"I've never missed anyone so much in my life."

"I know you had things to do and I understand."

"Do you? There is so much I want to tell you that you need to know but..."

Marisa put her finger to Payton's lips. "Not now. That's not what I want to talk about."

"What do you want to talk about?"

"It doesn't really involve a lot of talking."

Marisa and Payton gathered up her things and they headed to the beach house.

Marisa led Payton to the stairwell that led directly up her bedroom's back patio deck, she dropped her things, including her wet Levi shorts. She slipped inside through the patio door only wearing her wet, now see through, cotton panties.

Payton followed like a moth to the flame. At the end of the bed he dropped his back pack on the ground, took Marisa in his arms, and kissed her so tenderly restoring his faith that their passion for one another had never wavered. He needed her, and also needed to tell her so much more, but his desire to please her came first. With his hands holding her face, he gently pulled her close and kissed her once again. "Now what didn't you want to talk about?"

Marisa felt that kiss in every part of her as a breath of life to her soul. With her eyes still shut, she felt Payton brush his left thumb across her cheek, then across her lips. She opened her mouth slightly and allowed the end of his thumb to slip inside her mouth and she welcomed it as her lips closed around it. Slowly pulling his thumb from her mouth, he brushed the wetness across her dry lips, moistening them then kissed her once more.

"Payton, you've opened my eyes to a whole new world and as much as I've wanted to run away, I needed you to come back to me even more."

Payton slid his hand up along her right side and as

he caressed her, he could feel her begin to tremble with anticipation in his arms. She drew a deep sigh from his mouth while his touch caused her breasts to rise and fall as she put her hand over his, taunting and inviting one another to explore.

Payton felt the rush of everything that had happened come roaring back, "I'm no good for you, Marisa."

"Don't say that. It's over, you can get out now.

"You say that like I have a choice."

"You do have a choice and I'm standing right in front of you."

Marisa slid her hand down across his chest, down his firm six-pack, then undid his belt. She pulled out the bottom of his shirt and pulled it up over his head, letting it fall where it may.

"The truth is..."

Marisa saw Payton's eyes begin to swell with tears of such true emotion and she wanted to take away his pain. She kissed him with every part of her being, "The truth is, you gave me back my life and I want to return the favor."

"You don't understand. I've done a lot of bad

things."

"As long as you love me, you're forgiven."

Payton felt the torment between the truth and the lies he would have to bear. Marisa slipped her hands into the back of his jeans, her hands continued to run down over his firm backside, as she brushed his jeans away and let them fall. Payton didn't take his eyes off of Marisa as he stepped out of his jeans. With each kiss, another moment in time captured. Payton dropped to his knees and wrapped one arm around her waist and the other a bit lower just under her ass cheeks as if he was going to lift her, but instead he just held her tight. He prayed she could forgive him for the truth that laid just below the surface of his heart as he rested the side of his face along her tummy. Her skin was so warm and soft, unlike the three day stubble he had that didn't seem to bother Marisa. He could smell her skin and the light scent of the coconut oil she must have put on earlier that blended with her natural scent that was calling to him. He sat her back onto the edge of the bed and kissed her knee as she watched him rub his cheek against her inner thigh. She felt her leg twitch as he kissed her three times up along the inner portion of her long, gorgeous legs as he reached his destination.

Feeling the anticipation that was met with even more than she remembered, Marisa gripped and held onto the edge of the bed. Payton rubbed his face right above her love triangle, then off to one side, closer to her hip, and hit that nerve just right. She put her hand on the back of his head and uncontrollably tensed her stomach muscles.

Payton felt Marisa wrap her leg around his shoulder as her heel dug into his back. The evening sunset broke through the thin lace yellow patio curtains and cast a shadow of their silhouettes on the far wall. The image of the lovers entwined enhanced the already golden glow to the room. Payton slid up her body leaving meaningful delicate kisses, tasting the passion that poured from her bronzed skin. His hands led the way and they flowed up Marisa's body as she lay back onto the bed. He brushed the back of his hand lightly across her cheek, back down along her neck, and to her breast. He felt her arousal as each finger slowly glided across, flicking her tender nipple. She arched her back as she felt Payton's mouth kiss the lusciousness of her breast.

Payton could feel her heartbeat in the palm of his hand and it felt like a thunder that powered its way across a dark stormy sky.

Marisa crept out from under Payton and worked herself up onto the center of the bed. Payton crawled up after her like the panther of his persona evoked. Marisa rolled him over so she could be on top and as she straddled him, she ran her hands up and down over his lean muscular torso, through his dark rich chest hair, and dug her nails into him.

Marisa made her declaration, "You're never going to leave me again. Where you are right now, in my arms, this is your home."

"Marisa..."

"Just love me, Payton."

Payton's hands could not get enough of caressing Marisa and she was just fine with that. He reached up and took her breasts in his hands, she grabbed onto his wrists and guided his hands down, placing his hands onto her hips as she began to rock her body over him. Payton slid his hands back around her waist and took hold of her hips. He helped her to grind and gave her something to push back against, which gave her more control to feel him beneath her. They both felt the urgency even stronger as Payton sat up, Marisa reached down and guided Payton inside her.

Time did not exist. They were free to feel the constraints of reality fall away and just be there in the moment. Their passion for one another only grew and Marisa couldn't remember it ever being this good. It took the time apart to come to the understanding of knowing who she was so she could fully give herself to Payton. As they made love, he could feel her sweat gather on her back and run down her spine. His fingertips stimulated her already awakened senses as they followed the beads of passion that led down to the small of her back. He kissed her neck and felt transported by the taste of her sweat as the savory nectar that it was.

Marisa felt Payton so deep inside her and she couldn't get enough of him. They both felt Marisa start to slowly quiver. Payton wrapped his arms around her with such devotion, she never felt safer in her life and was able to let go completely. Payton felt her give herself to him and he too gave everything he had to her. When they came together, the intensity could only be matched by the energy and power of the surf as it pounded and crashed onto the ever changing shoreline.

The sun had long gone down but there was still enough light for Payton to make his way down stairs and bring back up some bottled water. He took a moment to look out the back slider onto the porch while he was down stairs. A slight breeze caused the sound of the waves crashing to alter the pitch but all in all a quiet night. He closed the door and headed back up. He took his strides up the weary steps of the old beach house. He remembered Marisa's words about no matter where he was, home was in her arms.

Marisa was lying on the bed propped up with a couple of pillows when Payton returned. He cracked open her water bottle and handed it to her. "Looks like these are the last two."

"We can go shopping tomorrow afternoon."

"I can go in the morning."

"No, you can't. You not going anywhere."

"About that. We have to talk Marisa. There is a lot I have to tell you."

Marisa had a good idea from the postcards what Payton had to do to clear his name and remove Delgado, removing the final threat on her life. But his eyes said there was something more and what is was she had no idea.

In the silence, they both heard it. The stairs that led up to her room from inside the house, squeaked.

Payton put his finger to his lips and mouthed the words, "Do you trust me?"

Marisa nodded.

Payton grabbed his backpack off the floor, unzipped it, and pulled out a silenced .22 and a bullet proof vest. He pulled Marisa out of the bed and then turned on the shower only using the hot water to create as much steam as he could.

While Payton was down stairs he had left the sliding door unlocked. Even though Payton had eliminated Delgado and his associates, the one person who was still unaccounted for was Mia. He knew she would never give up and the only way to draw her out and force her to expose herself was to bring her to Marisa. It wasn't Payton who had been observing Marisa on the beach that day, it was Mia, waiting for Payton to show...and he did.

Mia approached the bedroom door, saw it was slightly open, and could hear the shower running. She used the end of the silencer on her Beretta to slowly push the door open. She saw Payton in the bed facing away.

Payton had slid open the curtains on the back sliding glass door enough to see a reflection of Mia as she cautiously began to enter the bedroom.

Payton wanted Mia to focus on him, "Marisa, save me some hot water, would ya!"

Piff. Piff. Mia shot Payton in the back with two rounds. Payton didn't move.

Mia took a few steps inside and headed for the bathroom. The shower was dimly lit and the stream made it hard to see clearly. Mia felt the heat of the thick air and it was like a sauna, way too hot to shower in, but that realization was too late. When Mia had entered, she really hadn't noticed the closet door being half open. Marisa was stepping out of the closet with Payton's silenced .22. Mia looked to her right and saw her own reflection in the sliding glass doors, she also saw Payton eyes watching her every move, and then she saw Marisa pointed the .22 in her direction. Mia whirled and Marisa fired three rounds into Mia. Piff. Piff. Piff.

Payton spun out of bed wearing his bulletproof vest. He knew Mia well enough she would go for center mass. Mia was hanging on to life when she looked at Marisa, "Did he tell you?" She coughed up a little blood. "That he killed your parents?"

Marisa looked at Payton and was looking for a denial but his silence and distance only confirmed what Mia had asked. "Is it true Payton?"

Payton's heart sank and although his lips could not form the words Marisa needed to hear, she saw the pain in his face. As if a curse he carried was lifted, the tears that harbored the truth were evident.

Piff. Marisa fired one round into the center of Payton's vest sending him backwards onto the bed. He was able to sit up and slowly get to his feet. Marisa lowered the gun to her side.

From the floor Mia saw enough to know Payton had given Marisa the means to handle herself. "I didn't think you had it in you."

Piff. Piff. Marisa had to only swing the .22 out a foot or so to have a bead on Mia and capped her off with two final rounds. "Well, now you know."

Marisa's pain was only matched by her anger if what Mia said was true. The man she gave her deepest love to just hours before was standing right in front of her wishing for one day he could take back.

Marisa needed to know. "I just killed for you. You owe me the truth."

Payton had been holding this burden for so long. He took it as his penance to save Marisa's life for the one order he had followed blindly. Not thinking of who's lives he was going to change, but was only acting out of his desire to save the life of the only other woman he had ever loved, Kate.

"I'm sorry, Marisa."

Piff. Another round to the center of the vest. Payton was slammed back into the wall. As much as it hurt, he felt it had to be less pain than what Marisa was feeling right now.

Payton confessed, "You know now, your husband was the nephew of General Delgado and what happened to Kate and me. I was asked to do many things I'm not proud of in order to have the chance to get her back alive. One of those assignments was to fix the brakes on your car and when you survived the accident, Robert had asked your parents to come out to see you here in L.A. He even offered to fly them out, but when your father insisted on flying out his personal plane, Robert saw the opportunity to wipe away the history with your family clean once and for all. He assigned me to tamper with the engine of his plane, to make it fail, and I did."

Payton could see Marisa's world was being turned upside down and he stopped. Marisa pointed the .22 at Payton to continue.

"Then when I saw you in Robert's office that day and you couldn't pull the trigger, it hit me, not only was he using you, he was using me to get to you and you didn't deserve any of this. I knew then I wasn't going to kill you. Instead, I would risk my life in order to save you, and in the process, I found myself falling in love with you and I knew one day I would have to pay for what I had done."

Payton removed the bullet proof vest and tossed it on the bed. He looked at Marisa now as a woman no longer under anyone's shadow and himself as a man who no longer had a misguided sense of morality. He thought by telling her, he would have lifted the burden off his chest but he still felt it would be there forever. A reminder of the man he no longer wanted to be.

Marisa raised the gun at Payton. "You never once said you were sorry."

"Sorry is not enough to express how I feel."

"Did you ever really love me or was it a part of your master plan for forgiveness?"

Payton had risked his life to protect her and now he stood there willing to die for her in order to prove his point. "You tell me."

Everything Marisa had been through was now at the end of her finger tip. She had the man who changed her life forever, either to love or to kill… Dead to Rights.

Made in the USA
San Bernardino, CA
07 July 2017